BOYCHICK

With Narration By
Langameintza "The Shpeiler"

Written by Richard L. Decof

BOYCHICK

With Narration By
Langameintza "The Shpeiler"
Written by Richard L. Decof

Published by Amazon/Kindle
September, 2019

Expanded edition
June, 2020

THE BOYCHICK STORIES

APPENDIX

SOMETIME

He gets these thoughts in his head. He doesn't know why they appear, or where they come from. Suddenly.... unexpected, unplanned, off-the-wall, creative thoughts are just there. The most amusing of all came to him a few weeks after the Touch Football game - a summer Sunday afternoon lounging alone in the Big Field.

First Harold “Boychick” Silverman swore he saw a line of tanks approaching over the ridge of First Avenue hill and across the field toward him. At least a company of heavily-armed combat soldiers followed closely behind the tanks, weaving side-to-side to avoid any incoming fire, staying low in the tall grass for camouflage. As suddenly as they appeared, the tanks and soldiers became heat vapor, vanishing without a trace.

Boychick liked the direction this was going in...some fine summer Sunday afternoon dreaming. He rolled over on his back to dream some more.

“It's Sometime,” he thought..."but it's the kind of Sometime you haven't seen for awhile....”

"It's the kind of summer Sometime that makes desert cacti look up and say, 'How 'bout some rain?' Old Sol just looks back hotter at them. They all sigh and nudge closer together for shade."

"It's the kind of lemon meringue Sunday Sometime that's quiet, but you know everything's got to be exciting because nothing's going on."

"It's a silent Sometime, and the alpha wolves howl to let the others know they've caught food for the pack. They all come down from the rocks slowly, trying not to burn their pads on the hot boulders."

"It's a steamy Sometime fit for little green lizards that dart between the rocks, turning brown when they reach shade, which is hardly at all."

The steamy Sometime heat took the shape of native teepees wavering in the vapors, then bursting into flames. He imagined uniformed men on horseback shouting "Hurray!", shooting their rifles into the air as the teepees disappeared.

Boychick felt sad at the thought of what was done to the American Indians. He was sure there were no Jewish men in Custer's cavalry, except maybe their lawyer.

He stared up at puffy white clouds in the blue summer sky. To Boychick these were fresh ponds full of wide-mouth bass, swimming through the air thousands of feet above.

Boychick's was a strange convoluted creative mind that danced with reality, but changed partners often. It was a four-walled racquetball court kind of mind with little blue rubber ideas bouncing in all directions.

His mind was a dense jungle, filled with wild animals rambling through colorful tropical foliage choked with thick weeds. It was an intense LSD mind-trip, where every motion trailed off into purple and orange, and the concepts which made sense became ice, only to melt in the summer heat.

It was an alphabet mind with 26 letters in any order it chose that day. It was a Boychick mind.

THE UNTIMELY DEATH OF RHODA LANGAMEINTZA

New Jersey, 1980

My family name is Langameintza, which in Yiddish means long story. Pardon my accent - I vasn't born here in America.

Neighbors and friends call me "The Shpeiler", an honorary Yiddish title meaning storyteller. Stories are my passion and my pleasure… only quality, no drek... you'll see.

I'm a widower, now nearly 70 years old. You would know me - glasses, thinning gray hair, potbelly, varicose veins -- the whole gashmeer. What can you do when you get old? Your feet go bad… you grepps after every meal. An old man still has his stories.

Thirty years I've watched over this suburban neighborhood from my house near the top of First Avenue hill. Three blocks below is General MacArthur Boulevard, the local 7-11 and Greenberg's Meat Market.

Such a nice view! From my back porch I can see almost three square miles of north Jersey. From my front window I can see and hear nearly everything that happens in this neighborhood ...not that I'm watching or listening.

For many years I shared this house with my late wife Rhoda, may she rest in peace. Awful death, my Rhoda, but a quick end with little suffering.

I should talk nicer about those who've passed on, but the last few years with Rhoda was mostly "Yak yak yak yak." Every day another tsimis. You could have platzed from the aggravation. Still I loved that woman. What I wouldn't give for just one more argument!

Rhoda's departing at the youthful age of 48 was such a tragedy you shouldn't know. She died of wonton-soup-strangulation in the Happy Canton Restaurant. This from a woman who could pass a gallstone without wincing, but obviously could not swallow a wonton whole.

I looked over the duck sauce and silk roses and asked her, "Rhoda, nudnik, what's your problem? You're making a scene!" She never answered me. The woman would turn blue before she would give you a straight answer to a question.

"Fine then," I said. "Don't answer me. Finish your soup before it gets cold."

But Rhoda got cold before the soup. Who knew? She made some desperate gasping noises, then fell off her chair, sprawled out on the red plaid carpet, the wonton lodged in her throat.

Two waiters tried to revive her while Madame Chin dialed 911. A courageous effort, but too late, my Rhoda was gone. You should pardon I didn't read her fortune cookie.

THE BIRENBAUMS

So now I'm a widower in this quiet neighborhood. Quiet, that is, until the retired couple next door, decided to sell their home.

I wish you could have met the Birenbaums. What a pleasure having nice elderly neighbors like them - no trash, no loud noises, manicured yard.

Mrs. Birenbaum loved to cook holiday meals and bake pastries. Oh, the delicious smells that came from that kitchen! She made the best Chocolate Babka in all of north Jersey.

Every year at Pesach she would bring me Mandel Bread and a box of that delicious babka. Such a balaboosta! Butter wouldn't melt in that woman's mouth. Always a warm friendly smile and the bright twinkle in her eyes. Between just us, I have to be honest - her tuchas was a little zaftig.

Mr. Birenbaum was, sad to say, elderly and infirm. He was older than his wife by at least ten years, the exact number he never told me. His tall frame had become slightly stooped and I thought a bit too thin from the Diabetes. He wore professorial spectacles which made him resemble the ex-President Woodrow Wilson.

Birenbaum and I dovened together on holidays since he couldn't get to shul. His retirement was mostly spent in a worn overstuffed living room chair reading a book, or reviewing a stamp album from his collection. On the dining room table he assembled jigsaw puzzles with thousands of pieces.

Once in a while he would call me to play Canasta and maybe drink a shot of bourbon with a ginger back.

"Langameintza," he would say. "Sit with me in the dining room. Have a little drink and help me with this puzzle." I always obliged. The drink made him feel younger for a minute or so.

Birenbaum's health was failing but his mind had not lost a step. The old man had a long career as a corporate tax accountant - very sharp with the numbers. Well into his 80s, he could still add a column of numbers in his head as you shouted them out – a walking adding machine in support hose and corrective shoes. In our years as neighbors I figure he saved me more than $2000 on my returns. Not a paltry sum in those days.

In 1961, both Birenbaums decided they were not able to care for themselves. They lived off his pension, and thanked Roosevelt for the monthly Social Security, but there were no children or grandchildren to visit them.

The time had come. They sold their house and moved to the Jewish Home For The Aged where they comfortably lived out their remaining years. I visited him weekly until he died, and still see her, although she doesn't remember me so well anymore.

Enough about the past. I'm rambling when I should be getting to the point. The shpeil I want to tell you isn't about me, or the Birenbaums, or Sadie Moscowitz's left elbow. None of that would fill two pages and you'd be asleep by the end of one,

My story is about the mashugana kid that was born in the Birenbaum house who turned the neighborhood upside-down and captured my heart. Now that's a story with laughter and pathos. That's a story you can shake your head and say, “Unbelievable this kid! What a Boychick!”

That actually became his nickname, but I'm getting ahead of myself.

DAVE AND LYNN SILVERMAN HAVE A SON

I was lonely, first without my Rhoda, and then also the Birenbaums. That all changed when a young couple, Dave and Lynn Silverman, bought the Birenbaum house next-door.

The day they moved in, my new neighbors stopped over to say hello. They brought grocery-store babka but (I will translate from Yiddish) "The gift is not as precious as the thought".

A nice young couple, the Silvermans - a good match. In Hebrew we call such a match "Bashert" which means "meant to be" or some say "written in stone with the finger of God."

Lynn is an intelligent, petite, attractive brunette with a warm smile, interesting conversation and always a lovely peck on the cheek for me, both coming and going.

Her husband Dave is also smart and friendly. He works long hours selling mens' clothes - a fine business. In Yiddish we say (I'll translate) "A craft is a kingdom!"

Dave Silverman always warmly shakes

my hand, coming and going, with a "very glad to see you". Nice boy. Enormous hands.

These were hamisha people my new neighbors, ready to start a family, and that didn't take long.

Harold Abram Silverman was born in 1962 in the house next door formerly owned by the Birenbaums. Even as a tiny baby Harold had no patience.

Unlike many first-time mothers, Lynn enjoyed being pregnant. The awkward walk and occasional discomfort didn't bother her much. She wasn't by nature a complainer. Her days were filled with cooking, knitting and household chores.

From my front porch I often heard Lynn playing classical music record albums... not that I'm listening. Since her husband Dave worked long hours at the clothing store, Lynn stopped by often to chat, always with a sweet strudel or a box of rugelach in her hands.

She told me she hoped by playing the music recordings near her pregnant belly her baby might find music in his life.

Now it was nearly time. Lynn's belly was enormous. For a day or two she mentioned she felt mild twinges. Somehow she knew the baby wasn't quite ready yet.

When the twinges came again, Lynn barely said "Boo" when her water suddenly burst. Before their rotary phone could dial 911, the kid plopped out healthy, kenahora.

(I'll translate from Yiddish) "With a child in the house, all corners are full."

THE LEGEND OF HARUL

Dave and Lynn Silverman chose the name “Harold” to honor Dave’s maternal grandfather Harul, a Ukrainian farm boy who emigrated to America in the 1890s. For the baby’s Hebrew name they chose "Avram", the name Biblical Abraham was originally given at birth.

Family legend says Harul was drafted into the Cossacks, the Czar's cavalry. At first he enjoyed wearing the uniform, caring for the horses, and eating steady meals, but missed his family and hated sleeping outside.

Most Cossacks were goyim or descendants of Mongols, so Harul slept rarely and with one eye open. Jews were not well loved in 1890 Russia or any other time.

During a violent battle with fierce Poles, Harul decided the military was no place for a peace-loving Jewish boy. The next morning when the Cossacks rode west toward another battle, Harul hid under animal feed in a farmer's barn, then rode south.

Many weeks later, tired and hungry, he reached the Black Sea port of Odessa, where he found work as a crewman on a ship bound for England and then America.

For the rest of his life, Harul told anyone who would listen about entering New York Harbor and his first sight of the Statue Of Liberty.

"Liberty, she vas so huge… so beautiful. She called to me saying, 'Harul you are free here in America. No more Cossacks. No more Czars. You haf a new life. Is okay to be American and be a Jew.'"

Every year until his death Harul visited the Statue.

GOD WAS WITH THIS MAN

Every shetyl (town) needs a house of worship which becomes also a social center for Jewish families. In this town it's Temple Beth-Shalom, which was founded 80 uears ago by Mordecai Silverman, Dave Silverman's paternal grandfather. That friends, is the making of a fine shpeil.

Temple legends tell us that Rabbi Mordecai Silverman was a learned Orthodox rabbi with a flaming red beard and a fiery oratory which left everyone spell-bound. His congregation believed that God was with this man.

As a young rabbi, Mordecai led a congregation in the town of Grubna in western Russia near Moldavia. The newly-appointed mayor of Grubna was fearful of these black-coated Jews with their long beards and their strange Hebrew and Yiddish languages.

On orders said to be from the Czar himself, this mayor closed Grubna's synagogue and jailed the few protesters. Word spread that the rabbi was to be hanged.

Worshippers quickly packed Mordecai's books and meager possessions, and spirited the rabbi and his family out of town. The frightened family barely escaped with their lives. Two of Mordecai's seven children did not survive the rough voyage.

A year later, a blessing, a healthy boy. Rabbi Mordacai named his baby son Morris, a variant of Moses which means "I drew him out of the water." The family had crossed an ocean so that Morris could be born an American citizen.

Rabbi Mordecai Silverman spurned the potential adoration of a New York City congregation, preferring the quiet of northern New Jersey. It was here that he founded Temple Beth-Shalom which now, 80 years later, numbers 500 families.

Mordecai blessed the first foundation block, but died before the temple was finished. Popular legend says that God came for this holy man just as he came for Moses before the Israelites reached the Promised Land. Only the Silverman family (and your Shpeiler) knows that the rabbi died in the arms of an admiring shayna maidel.

Aged members of the congregation still lower their voices to a whisper and touch the bronze letters as they pass Rabbi Mordecai Silverman's nameplate on the Temple's memorial wall.

Rabbi Mordecai Silverman spurned the potential adoration of a New York City congregation, preferring the quiet of northern New Jersey. It was here that he founded Temple Beth-Shalom which now, 80 years later, numbers 500 families.

Mordecai blessed the first foundation block, but died before the temple was finished. Popular legend says that God came for this holy man just as he came for Moses before the Israelites reached the Promised Land. Only the Silverman family (and your Shpeiler) knows that the rabbi died in the arms of an admiring shayna maidel.

Aged members of the congregation still lower their voices to a whisper and touch the bronze letters as they pass Rabbi Mordecai Silverman's nameplate on the Temple's memorial wall.

MISHPOCHA

Most American Jews can only trace their family's history to a grandparent or great-grandparent who immigrated before 1900. They may also know about a town in Russia or Poland, but not much more.

Dave Silverman was luckier than most. Though he never met his grandparents, Dave's family history contained many colorful stories about his mother Raisa's father Harul and of course Morris's father Rabbi Mordecai Silverman.

Lynn knew very little about her family lineage. Her father Ben related what stories he remembered from childhood about the many fine Temples, the busy central marketplace and the popular Yiddish theatres of urban Bialyshtok.

Hundreds of years earlier bubonic plague devastated much of Europe's population. As a result Jews were invited to work the many vacant farms and estates in Eastern Europe.

By the mid 1800s, a person could travel from Latvia or Estonia in the north to Moldavia in the south, always finding Jewish communities that spoke Yiddish.

In March 1881 when Jews were blamed for the murder of Russia's Czar Alexander, it was no longer safe to travel freely or live in their shtetls. The Great Migration to America began.

All four of Boychick's grandparents were born in America. For Jews, being born in America signified a new start in a hopefully safe country… again.

Lynn Silverman's parents, Esther and Ben lived in the next town. They were friendly, involved, working-class Reform Jews thrilled to now have a grandson.

Esther was a traditional homemaker, gladly spending her life taking care of Ben. Now she found a higher purpose in being a grandmother, and cooking delicious dinners for the family on Jewish holidays.

Dave Silverman's parents, Raisa and Morris, were amiable, but could also be somewhat aloof. Both were raised in an Orthodox section of Brooklyn where social skills were quite secondary to faith. Their humor was droll, their lifestyle simple and their cooking a bit tasteless.

Jewish children of that early 1900s generation, including all 4 of Boychick's grandparents, spoke Hebrew in Temple, Yiddish at home, and English in the street to blend in with America as much as possible.

Esther lost her mother when she was only five years old. At fifteen her father married an intolerant older woman. Esther's sister made room and found her a retail job.

The millinery store paid Esther three dollars a week, which was a livable wage in 1920. One dollar helped her sister pay the rent. Another dollar was saved for a time when, God forbid, she might be out of work and need her savings. The third dollar she spent frugally on her own needs.

"Spend a little, save a little, have a little." she would say.

When they met, Grandpa Ben worked in a five-and-dime store. He was a dashing youth - a sporty dresser with a fashionable straw hat and a diamond pinky ring.

His hypnotic blue eyes and charming demeanor totally disabled Esther. She married him as soon as her sister deemed it appropriate, but never could understand why such a handsome gentleman would marry such a monkey-face.

Ben always counted his lucky stars that he found such a wonderful, loving, caring woman to share his life.

Dave Silverman rarely got to see his parents. Raisa (Harul's daughter) and Morris Silverman (Rabbi Mordecai's youngest son) lived down south in Florida. Soon after their wedding in 1930, Morris and Raisa Silverman rented a 4th floor walk-up apartment in the Orthodox section of Brooklyn.

In summer the small apartment became a steamy sweat-box with paint peeling off the rough plaster walls. In winter, frozen breezes leaked through every window. Iron radiators clanked and banged all night as the hot water flowing inside expanded and contracted the metal ribs.

Morris kvetched constantly. He hated living in crowded noisy dirty expensive New York City.

One evening shortly after the Second War, Morris came home with the deed to a Florida apartment which he had won in a poker game.

"Raisa, pack your things. Say goodbye to this New York crap furniture and the three locks on the door... we're moving to Miami Beach."

She didn't argue. Raisa grabbed young David, threw what she could carry into the Buick, and they headed south on Route One. Four days later they were Floridians forever.

THE BRIS

Langameintza, your Shpeiler here. Sorry to intrude, but I'm getting shpilkas waiting to tell you about the baby's bris. Was I invited you ask? I should answer such a question?

In a previous shpeil, I told you Harold Silverman was born in 1962 to my hamisha next-door neighbors David and Lynn. Eight days later he was already causing problems.

Baby Harold almost didn't have a bris. His first week of life had been peacefully quiet, in an upstairs bedroom, only attended by his mother, father and grandparents.

Now, a week later, the entire mispocha had gathered to kvell over the new baby... and were they noisy!

Lynn's mother Esther - a kindly genuine balabusta - planned every detail of the Bris and played hostess. Her husband - portly, personable and somewhat mischievous Grandpa Ben - greeted guests and did any necessary introductions.

Dave's mother and father drove up from Florida. They were easily recognizable with their dark bronzed skin and brightly colored tropical clothing. Morris and Raisa were both exuberant at becoming grandparents.

After the necessary niceties, Lynn's sister Zelda parked herself in a position to command the room's attention, conducting audiences with guests as if she was royalty.

Chips and dip, soft drinks, and napkins were brought to her. Her dirty plates were removed on request. With her hunger satisfied, she began reading a book. As her new nephew was carried in for the Bris ceremony to begin, Zelda fell asleep in her chair, snoring loudly.

The tiny 8-day-old baby must have been frightened by the noise, the smells and all the unfamiliar people in the crowded Family Room. When Harold was handed to the mohel, he probably wondered who is this scary bearded adult dressed in black. Why is he trying to remove that diaper?

Baby Harold sensed that something he wouldn't like was about to happen so he adamantly refused to cooperate.

On the first and second attempts to begin the ceremony, as the Mohel removed the diaper, baby Harold released any liquids and waste in his system.

The third time the tiny 8-day-old baby messed in his diaper, Mohel Eliyahu Ben-Zion shouted something Hebrew in the air, then stormed out of the room, his tallit following closely in the breeze behind him.

Dave's best friend, “Uncle Max”, volunteered to fix the situation. Max smoothed the mohel’s feathers with a crisp $20 bill and a new joke the mohel could tell the audience.

This time the baby was dry, the joke was funny and the foreskin came right off.

“May this little mashugana live long and prosper, kenahora.”

MY RESUME AS A SHPEILER

It's only right I should list for you my qualifications as a Shpeiler, since you're trusting me to tell this story properly, You expect quality storytelling, not a bunch of drek from an alte-kocker.

Therefore, I submit to you my three finest works as a Shpieler - my marriage proposal, my draft dodge and my sales pitch. **Then** you'll know that Langameintza is no ordinary storyteller – no **schlepper** just off the boat.

Back in 1930, in Brooklyn, I proposed to my Rhoda. She more or less said yes.

I asked "Will you marry me?"

Typically Jewish, she answered the question with a question, "Will I marry you?"

That night I convinced her mother, her father, her two maiden sisters and Aunt Ida the Mavin that I was a hard-working young man with a proper Jewish background. I would take such good care of their Rhoda they shouldn't ever get a call or a worry.

How I kept a straight face through that night I'll never know, Six fish without hardly baiting the hook. While I was on a roll, I talked Rhoda's father into paying for the wedding. A natural born shpeiler? Wait… it gets better.

During World War 2, the Army tried to draft me. I was in my early 30s, still living in Brooklyn, selling carpet remnants to people who couldn't afford better and collecting every week on the balance.

In those days we did what we could to earn a living. It was honest work. I was proud of my job and my rugs.

Hard-working families sacrificed one day of their month's salary to have nice carpet remnants in their home, It made them feel successful.

Every day I walked my route until my feet wore out the soles of my shoes. Oy… were my poor feet a mess! At night I soaked those sore, tired feet in hot water and Epsom Salts until I felt some relief, if ever. Always I went to sleep with aching feet.

When the Army draft notice came, my Rhoda went meshugga. Like a fool, I would have gone. I wasn't born in America but this is my country and she's been good to me. Rhoda was adamantly opposed to my going.

"Think, Langameintza. What kind of soldier will you make? You'll grepps from the food, they'll make you work on Shabbos, and those feet of yours can't walk in shoes never mind march in boots. Tell them you have some disease. If you're half the storyteller you were at our engagement night you'll get yourself out of this.

Rhoda's real concern was herself. God forbid she should move back to her father's house with her maiden sisters and keep Kosher again. God forbid she should get a job so I could help free America from those Nazi bastards. So… for Rhoda's sake I told the Army a “meintza” – a story.

The day before reporting to the military I walked my collection route as usual. Oy, my feet were bright red, aching and peeling that night. This time I just stood the pain and went to bed.

Next morning I reported for my Army physical. While the military doctor was examining my sore peeling feet, I dropped a large piece of skin on the floor, a thoughtful gift from my friend Benny the Undertaker.

“Nothing. Nothing.” I told the doctor. “A little touch of Leprosy is all. It's in the early stages… nothing to be concerned about.”

I watched the doctor's horrified face absorb what he had just seen and the talented shpeil he had just heard.

"GET THIS 4F OUT OF HERE NOW!!!"

Such a shpeiler! Wait wait. I'm not done. One last item for the resume.

The carpet remnant route was a good job for a younger man. Rhoda suggested I find a retail job where the customers come to me, so I found work selling mattresses,

Turned out this was not just any sales job. The bigshot promoter in charge knew the owners of well-known furniture stores. Most were tired of the business or their money was tied up in merchandise. Some had idiot sons waiting daily for Dad to drop dead.

Nearly every owner was eager to make one last huge profit, shaft his idiot sons, then close forever and move to Miami.

This was BIG PROMOTION SALES EVENTS - lots of radio, newspaper and TV ads – each store packed to the gills with new stock brought in by the promoter. Trailer trucks loaded with inventory were lined up behind the store and daily manufacturer deliveries continually replaced what was sold.

Every sales event got rearranged for maximum success. The owner's existing inventory became a "Scratch and Dent" area at the store entrance, tagged "Discount - Priced To Go".

Behind the schlock furniture we arranged rows of sofas, love-seats, and recliners.

Dining rooms with hutches were set up along the walls, enhanced with realistic imitation oil paintings of fruit in baskets or French village street scenes.

At the rear of the store, where I worked, complete bedrooms were displayed with plastic-wrapped mattresses stood on end.

There was so much advertising, neon signs, banners and balloons! Even people who didn't need anything had to come take a look. Those customers bought the most.

We first started with a month or more of OWNER RETIRING SALE!, then turned it into a few weeks of LOST OUR LEASE SALE. Next it became an EVERYTHING MUST GO SALE!, heading all the time for the HUGE GIGANTIC GOING OUT OF BUSINESS SALE!!! A large clock in every newspaper ad reminded customers they were running out of time.

Once, after a snowstorm, part of the store's ceiling collapsed. Every local TV and radio station covered the disaster. For days the local newspaper ran updated versions of the tragedy. In reality only one sofa and a recliner were damaged, but the enormous free publicity started a Gold Rush. Who could complain? You know... I always wondered if the Sales Manager called the reporters. How did they know to all show up at once?

I was the “bedding specialist” since that job required the top notch schmoozing and closing.It was my pleasure and my income to “help” any customers who visited the back of the store.

“A good night's sleep on a comfortable mattress can change a person's life”, I would always say.

“Pardon me Mister, I want you should feel this mattress cover. Have you ever felt such soft rich texture? Here… lay down on the King Size. It's our finest bedding – 688 springs, all individually damask-wrapped, all hand-placed. The fabric is triple-sewn for long-lasting wear.” Such a shpeiler!

“These mattresses are custom made to our own specifications, at half the cost of brand names. Lay down with your husband Madam. Try this mattress out, you will love it. Oh, you're not married? I won't tell the Manager. He's very conservative. Will that be cash or charge?”

That shpeil sold a lot of mattresses. The sales manager always smiled when he handed out my check.

“Good job, Langameintza” he would say.

THE NICKNAME

Boychick's real name was Harold Abram Silverman, but friends and family called him "Boychick" since that Saturday at the beach when Grandpa Ben gave him the nickname.

On hot summer weekends, the Silvermans liked to take day-trips to the Jersey Shore. Lynn loved breathing salt air and feeling warm sand between her toes. She hoped the ocean breezes would ease little Harold's asthma. When Summer flowers bloomed, the pollen made it difficult for Harold to breathe.

Dave usually joined his wife and her mother Esther for long walks down the beach. Grandpa Ben preferred to lay on his lounge, spending quality leisure time with his grandson, little Harold. The genial old man and the clever little 3 year old had developed a communication not restricted to spoken language, which Harold was still learning. Smiles and winks often took the place of words.

When a shapely blonde in a brief bikini settled her towel near them, Grandpa's mischievous grin told the boy instinctively what to do. The old man winked at his grandson, then turned over on his back in the sand, seeming to choke.

Harold appeared to panic then ran straight to the nicely tanned blonde,

"Hep! Hep! My Gwanpa! PLEASE lady, PLEASE HEP!"

The blonde sprang into action, ran to Grandpa Ben and administered CPR. Over and over she blew into the old man's mouth while her oiled tan legs straddled his stomach.

In a few minutes the old man was revived, to the great relief of a small group of cheering onlookers. The heroine refused any reward, but accepted a grateful kiss and a little pat on the behind.

"I love this little Boychick!" Grandpa announced… and the name stuck.

GOOD ADVICE

Boychick's first chemistry kit at six destroyed the Bassett cherry dining room table. Two seemingly innocent ingredients in the kit blended to create a noxious compound which ate wood in seconds. The Silvermans thanked God and Prudential for their safety and their Homeowner's Insurance coverage.

His first puff of cigarette smoke at nine irritated Boychick's asthmatic lungs. As he coughed, he dropped both the glowing match and the lit cigarette on the Family Room carpet.

Orange flames quickly spread to the television then up the drapes. An emergency family bucket brigade passed a 5 quart plastic pail of water from the kitchen sink to the flames without much effect.

Firemen at the scene called the Family Room "a total loss". Prudential of New Jersey paid off again, then refused to renew their policy. Dave "The Pants Man" was furious.

"Max. You're my agent, my best friend. Come on buddy, help us out."

"Take my advice Dave. Get rid of the kid."

NOT FOR NOTHING

You see already, I'm a shpeiler, and a good one. As a young man, I fancied myself a writer - which is just a shpeiler with a bad memory. I wrote stories.... I wrote plays.... I wrote anything I could think of to get published - to get my big break in life.

My late wife Rhoda, may she rest in peace, always told me, "Langameintza, don't quit your day job." Lovely woman, my Rhoda. Such an encouraging positive lady. Storm clouds could have taken lessons from her on how to rain on parades.

How many cabs to Manhattan? How many fares did I pay so some goyishe-kop in a three-piece suit could tell me I'm an amateur – an upstart! - an unpublished nobody, **a nothing**!!! Did that Editor schmuck even read what I sent him? Did he look for the subtle nuances and the charming humor? Would anyone ever recognize the creativity, or sense the unique personality of Langameintza?

I'm a bitter old man that so far nobody knows the real Langameintza. Langameintza the poet. Langameintza the creative thinker. Langameintza the man. I'm just another face in the crowd with a prominent nose and a polite "How do you do? I'm fine thank you very much."

On the day that baby Harold Silverman was born, I vowed to capture in stories the essence of this boy. The world should know how precious and meaningful the life of one boy can be.

How do I know what happened? I live right next door.... my eyes are good… the house has windows. Not much gets past Mr. Langameintza… not that I'm snooping on neighbors.

Boychick is 18 now, graduated from high school, ready to leave for college. I, Langameintza was witness to it all - from birth to bris to first words to baby teeth to bicycle to Bar Mitzvah to now.

These stories are my memories - the ehmes. It's a long shpeil but a good one, though I may tell some parts out of order.

Langameintza doesn't usually write short stories any more and he doesn't write drek **ever**. Not for nobody. Only quality from your shpeiler - the whole megillah. My hope is you should remember this special boy.

Already I feel better. Now I'm warmed up and ready to tell you more about this mashugana kid next door. Pay close attention so I shouldn't have to repeat.

SISTER RUTHIE

Ruthie Silverman considered herself a lucky girl - a true survivor. She was born premature and undersized. Several times during early childhood Ruthie had again been hospitalized, but thanks to a strong will and constant family support, she always fought her way back to health. One illness, a respiratory condition, left her with a nasal voice which sounded like she was whining.

Despite health challenges and scrawny appearance, Ruth retained a strong independent stubborn will to do things herself – her way. She was grateful for her parents' affection, but was never needy or clingy with her father Dave or her mother Lynn.

Her brother Harold "Boychick" Silverman completely respected her wishes. He was her source of strength, a secret they kept to themselves.

Now nine years old, she was an awkward, gutsy, personable child. Kept mostly indoors, overprotected from allergies and any further sickness, Ruthie's skin had become pale and she was pitifully skinny. Her elbows protruded and her knees were boney.

A few cruel girls at Temple Beth-Shalom religious school taunted her as “meiskeit” - overlooked when God made beautiful. Even so, Boychick bonded with her from the very first day. He adored his little sister and would always protect her.

Harold “Boychick” Silverman was four years old the day his father Dave and exhausted happy mother Lynn walked in with his new baby sister. Ruthie had been born undersized and sickly, so she spent the first fourteen days of her life battling to stay alive.

At two weeks old baby Ruthie was still small and thin, but healthy enough to come home with her parents.

“Look Boychick, a miracle baby!” Lynn told him with a wide smile. “She's your sister Ruth. We named her after the strongest-willed woman in the Bible.”

To Boychick his new baby sister seemed so tiny… so delicate. After 14 days in Maternity Care his Mother appeared very tired, but also very happy.

“Her name means ‘friendship'. She's your sister, bubby… and your friend.”

In Yiddish we say “When a girl is born, it's a good omen for the family.”

Ruthie was a fighter - a survivor. The child had brains and guts too. From a very early age she demonstrated an adventurous inquisitive nature. What Ruthie lacked in beauty, she more than made up in intelligence.

Ruthie especially loved bedtime, when her mother read to her. Always the hands-on mother, Lynn took pride in personally instructing her clever children.

Every night Lynn read imaginative stories to her daughter and taught her the alphabet, as she had for her son at that age. Several times she found Ruthie studying a magazine or newspaper trying to sound out words.

Boychick had a talent for inventing games to play with his sister, beginning long before she could walk or talk. This was attention that little Ruthie loved,

They would crawl on the Family Room rug, barking like dogs or meowing like cats. Boychick would even lap milk from a bowl, which totally delighted his baby sister. When Lynn saw, she ended that game quickly,

"Sit at the table like mensch. Drink from a glass. Show your sister proper manners."

When Ruthie began pulling herself to her feet, Boychick helped his little sister learn to walk. As soon as Ruthie found mobility, she focused on riding her brother's skateboard - lying on it of course - pushing herself around with her toes, arms spread wide as if she was a bird. The kid was a pisser!

Some nights when Dave wasn't working in the clothing store, his friend Max would visit to discuss insurance and share funny stories. Max bought custom pants from Dave years ago, then Dave bought insurance from Max. Now they were so close that Boychick and Ruthie called him Uncle Max.

One Saturday, Uncle Max brought his daughter Jennifer to meet Ruthie. The two girls took an instant liking to each other.

They were the same age, height and weight, with families so close that the girls were practically cousins.

In public young Jennifer demonstrated the perfect manners she was taught - to always be cute, thoughtful and polite. In private she was a wily brash demonstrative child who hid nothing. The day they met, Jennifer asked Ruthie to be her best friend.

"I like you even though you have skinny

legs like a chicken."

Ruthie responded, "I like you too, even though your lips look like a fish."

The two girls stared at each with such seriousness, wondering if the other was offended. Then at once they both cracked up laughing, rolling over stuffed animals on the floor.

At times Ruthie abandoned logic. She had succeeded in conquering life-threatening diseases. Now she no longer had any sense of fear.

Her desire for adventure went beyond the thrill of riding roller-coasters or jumping into a swimming pool off the high diving board. This little girl's adventures could be dangerous. Boychick hoped he would always be there to rescue his little sister.

When the girls were six, Jennifer boldly challenged Ruthie to a skateboard race down First Avenue hill. The challenge was a bluff of course - blustering to gain respect.

Everyone in the neighborhood knew that First Avenue was a dangerous road, even for cars and bicycles. After the initial crest of the hill, the next three blocks descended at a steep angle, straight down to the 7-11 and Greenberg's Meat Market on MacArthur

Boulevard.

Ruthie considered the speed she might achieve racing down that steep hill on a skateboard. The element of danger was not an issue. Her only question was would it be fast enough to fly?

"I accept!"

While her brother and his friends were in the house pouring Gatorade, Jennifer and Ruthie borrowed two of their skateboards

"Bet you're chicken, chicken-legs" Jennifer taunted her friend.

"Bet I'm not, Fish-Lips", Ruthie snapped back. There was no fear in Ruthie's voice - she was excited.

Jennifer regretted every word of her challenge. She truly hoped Ruthie would give up the idea. An initial expression of curious wonder on Ruthie's face became that far-away dreaming look her brother Boychick displayed before each of his adventures.

"Let's do it."

The little girls dropped their borrowed skateboards on the sidewalk at the top of First Avenue hill. Ruthie was ready to go. Jennifer, all of a sudden, was not so sure.

"It's pretty scary, Ruthie. Let's go

home."

"Funny, Fish-Lips. Who's the chicken now?"

Both girls laid down on their stomachs on the skateboards. Their arms stretched out like wings for balance as they pushed forward. As their skateboards gained speed, they dropped over the crest of the hill. Now, nothing could stop their acceleration... It was 3 blocks straight down.

"Weeee… this is fun!"

At first Ruthie's long curly hair got in her eyes, then strands of curls floated behind her as the hill turned steeper. Her voice could barely be heard in the wind she created.

The speeding skateboard ride thrilled Ruthie. She already abandoned any worry about balance and began flapping her arms like a bird.

Ruthie shared Boychick's dream of flying. She had been in the station wagon the day her brother tried to impress their neighbor Audrey Rosen with his unsuccessful secret flight off the roof. His attempt landed painfully in the pricker bushes. Ruthie wanted to be the first in her family to actually fly.

"Ruthie, slow down!" Jennifer wet herself for the first time in 3 years.

Greenberg's Meat Market, at the bottom of First Avenue hill, was preparing to close for the day. Mr. Greenberg the butcher chose this exact moment to walk out to the sidewalk and discard the day's several large bags of trash.

Ruthie had no ability to steer her speeding skateboard. She clipped the butcher in the shins, spinning him totally around.

Now facing backwards, Mr. Greenberg was violently slammed by Jennifer as she and her skateboard raced by.

Trash and beef bones flew everywhere! Ruthie and Jennifer somehow continued on, across the Meat Market's parking lot, finally stopping safely in the butcher's shrubbery.

Dogs from around the neighborhood still bark in secret whispers about the day Mr. Greenberg, got dumped on his butt. So many bones!

As the butcher gained his senses, from out of nowhere appeared every collie, shepherd, dachshund, Saint Bernard, dalmatian, terrier and doberman. They eagerly pounced on the scattered beef bones.

At first, the neighborhood dogs were

mostly polite to each other, knowing there were more than enough bones to go around. A few of the fastest dogs ran to hide their first bone then return for another.

Big dogs fresh on the scene noticed others returning for "seconds". That's when the trouble started. Even dogs don't like a chazzer.

Aggressive barking turned into a loud, clawing, teeth-gnashing fight. Injured howling dogs ran away for their safety. Three badly injured neighborhood dogs were rushed to the Veterinary Hospital.

Hearing all the commotion, many nearby residents came out into the street, first to retrieve their dogs and later to help clean the butcher's parking lot.

Hours later, the scene had mostly calmed down. Neighbors were still in the street conversing with down-the-block friends they had all but forgotten about. Many were inviting each other to backyard barbecues, kvelling about their children and asking where has all that time gone since they saw each other last?

GIMME A SCHMEAR
(The Yiddish Conga Line)

It started with bagels, simple Saturday morning Bagels which naturally needed cream cheese. If Boychick and his sister Ruthie were well-behaved all week, their Saturday breakfast might include Nova or Whitefish and a slice of tomato.

Their father Dave “The Pants Man” had already left for work. Saturday was a big money day at the men's clothing store. The owner, Mr. Shapiro counted on Dave - his best salesman - to start early and stay late.

Grandpa Ben walked into the kitchen hungry for a fine Saturday breakfast. He preferred a few Old Country customs of respect. When the father wasn't home, Grandpa sat at the head of the table and waited to be served. His daughter Lynn didn't mind at all - in fact serving her father reflected her love and admiration. He asked for so little and gave their family so much.

As he chose his bagel, Grandpa Ben uttered the words which started that morning's chaos. He simply said “Gimme a schmear.”

Little Ruthie, now six years old, was at an age where she enjoyed both the meaning of words and the rhythm of speech. She found that Yiddish words were uniquely meaningful with a rhythm all their own.

In Ruthie's young creative mind, certain phrases became a song. Sharing her new song outloud was joyous fun. Ruthie proudly sang her grandpa's line to the family, first with a big smile, then a laugh, then ecstatic joy.

"Gimme a schmear."

"Gimme a schmear."

"Gimme a schmear."

Seeing his pale skinny sister so happy started ten year old Boychick repeating the line with her, singing in rhythmic unison:

"Gimme a schmear."

"Gimme a schmear."

"Gimme a schmear."

The children were having so much fun. Lynn and Grandpa Ben liked this game, so they decided to raise the ante.

Lynn asked "What about some Nova?"

Right away Ruthie, and then her brother Boychick picked up on the second line. Both children happily sang the new phrases in unison:

“Gimme a schmear. What about some nova?”

“Gimme a schmear. What about some nova?”

Boychick noticed that familiar wry smile and wink on Grandpa Ben's face and knew something delightful was coming next.

“Slice up some tomato. Let's all fress!”

Ruthie grinned from ear to ear as she quickly memorized the new lines. She nearly shouted, with her brother joining in:

“Gimme a schmear. What about some nova?” Slice up some tomato. Let's all fress.”

By now the children we're dancing around the room as they happily chanted. Grandpa Ben rose from his chair at the head of the table to join them, dancing in rhythm to their chants.

Lynn was overjoyed to see her family so happy.

“Oh my, Dad.... look at you!....CONGA LINE!!!”

Grandpa Ben led the parade around the kitchen table, followed by his daughter Lynn, then Boychick, then Ruthie. The children had never seen a conga line. They'd never seen their grandfather or their mother dancing.

Over and over everyone repeated the lines while parading around the kitchen table.

"Gimme a schmear. What about some nova?" Slice up some tomato. Let's all fress."

"Gimme a schmear. What about some nova?" Slice up some tomato. Let's all fress."

Finally Ben was exhausted. As he took his seat at the head of the table he began to speak, with Ruthie eagerly waiting for his next phrase.

Lynn rushed to quickly cover her father's mouth. He mumbled something that no one could understand (and Ruthie could not repeat).

Out of breath from the conga dance and the chanting, Lynn blessed them all.

"I'm quite happy to be in this family, Lynn told them, "Now no more talk. Eat your breakfast!"

AUDREY ROSEN
Part 1 - Audrey Had Skills

Harold “Boychick” Silverman was seven years old when the Rosen family moved in next door. All Boychick wanted to know for two days was did the new neighbors have any boys his age? He bothered Lynn day and night until she finally knocked on their door.

“They have a lovely seven year old daughter named Audrey”.

“Oh God, mom.” Boychick whined. “A girl!? I have to live next to a Audrey?”

Boychick decided to teach the new arrival who was boss on First Avenue Hill. He knocked on the Rosen’s door, introduced himself, and invited the new girl to “play”.

Audrey was the same age as Harold, but smaller and more athletic looking. Both of her knees we're skinned from daily skateboarding. She willingly followed her new friend outside, grateful to be away from helping her mother move in.

Boychick wanted to hate her, but didn't. He suspected that his new neighbor was no ordinary girl. Audrey had skills! Some proof of his dominance was required.

"Can you spit? Best spit over the street wins."

Loudly hocking up some phlegm, Boychick reared back, and spit it nearly across the street, almost to the curb. Satisfied with the distance, he glared at his female competitor with mild disgust ...after all, this was a boy's game.

Little Audrey didn't flinch. With certain bravada, she made a chuching noise equally as loud as he had done, then spit her saliva. The spitwad landed two feet farther than Boyhick's.

She glared triumphantly. Then a surprising matter-of-fact plain confident expression appeared on her face, which aggravated him more than any taunting or bragging.

"Lucky spit, girl. Bet you can't burp really loud like this"

Boychick swallowed gulps of air, then let fly a long loud grepps. He was very satisfied with his effort until he heard Audrey.

"BBBBBBBBBUUUUUUUUUURRRRRRRRR PPPPPPPPP!!!!!!"

Few boys and zero girls had ever beaten Boychick in a spitting contest or a burping contest. Frustrated, he reacted, firmly pushing this new smirking girl on her butt. Boychick figured his point had been made.

Audrey wasn't accepting this abuse at all. She jumped up looking quite ferocious, and picking up a lump of clay, she heaved it at Boychick s face.

The lump happened to have a rock in it which split his upper lip and knocked out both of his front teeth. From this first meeting Boychick developed a healthy respect for Audrey Rosen.

AUDREY ROSEN
Part 2 - Write Me A Song

Despite taunting comments from friends at school, Boychick and Audrey became friends. Some afternoons she would stand in his front yard, just outside the Living Room windows, teasing him about his piano lessons.

Boychick and his parents mutually agreed that for him to succeed at piano he should come straight home after school to practice for an hour. Now that the days were longer and the weather better, he regretted that agreement.

Lynn knew her son was talented but lazy. Boychick needed to be trained, scheduled, and if necessary whipped to learn. He wanted to just play ball after school like other kids which made him defensive about playing the piano.

His current practice assignment was an exercise from Czerny's "The School Of Velocity". Starting at the lowest A, he played two-handed scales up the entire length of the keyboard then back down.

After each completed scale set, he raised up one half note higher and repeated the pattern. Each musical key required attention to its unique fingering and crossovers for smooth transitions.

"Can you hear me Boychick? It's Audrey. Come out and play."

Audrey knew he had to practice piano after school. She was taunting him.... tempting him.

"We're all going to The Big Field to play kickball."

Audrey naturally teased Boychick all the time like any other little girl, but she had no bad intentions. She actually liked him.

(Sound of two-handed scales in D Major, ascending oblongata up and down the piano keyboard.)

"I know you can hear me, Mozart. Learn to play well so you can write me a song."

Boychick raised his scale pattern to E-flat major and continued, trying to ignore the pesky little girl.

"Go play with your friends, Audrey, Boychick has to practice."

Turning to her son Lynn added, “And you, Mr. Leonard Bernstein wanna-be, continue your scales and ignore your girlfriend.”

“MOMMMMM! She's not my girlfriend.”

As he practiced, he couldn't stop thinking about what Audrey had just said. A feeling of unexpected warmth came over him. Someday he would write that song and play it for her. From then on he was never ashamed about the piano.

AUDREY ROSEN
Part 3 - THE SECRET FLIGHT

Mr. Langameintza, your Shpeiler, interrupting, I know, but for good cause. I heard the commotion that day. I saw what I saw and told nobody.

No, I wasn't prying or spying.... I'm not that way. I live right next door ...the window was open on a nice day. An old man has little to do besides count his toes and waste away in front of the television. Okay, so I was watching the young people. So sue me.

It was a clear brisk April Wednesday afternoon in north Jersey. A slight breeze seemed to gain strength as it crested First Avenue Hill then brushed tall grass in The Big Field where neighborhood children play after school.

Precocious fifth-grade Audrey Rosen and her neighbor "Boychick" Silverman had resolved their initial childhood differences and were now good friends.

After school all Boychick could talk about was flying. Boychick was obsessed with a kite his Grandpa Ben gave him, and a Japanese Zero fighter-plane model his father helped him glue together.

Audrey ran upstairs to her room to change clothes. She could hear Boychick's daily piano practice ritual, carried on the breeze from the Silverman living room. He always warmed up with two-handed scales in every key, followed by arpeggios.

Today he followed with a Bach Invention. Even at 10 years old Boychick's piano playing often made her smile, but she would never reveal that secret… or any secret.

Reviewing her closet, Audrey selected a cute denim jumpsuit. Her second floor bedroom was on the side facing Boychick's house. By standing next to her white French provincial canopy bed she could see into Boychick's bedroom window.

"What a nice Spring day" she thought to herself. Then Audrey noticed all was quiet. Boychick's piano practicing had stopped.

As she fastened her jumpsuit straps, Audrey saw a boy's sneaker roll down the Silverman's roof. Then another sneaker rolled off the roof, dropping into the bushes.

Audrey moved closer to her canopy bed for a better look, nearly knocking her frilly white lamp off the nightstand. She was just in time to witness Harold on the roof of his house, flapping his arms, preparing to fly.

Imitating her mother's voice, she told herself, “My mashugana friend has finally lost what mind he had.”

With her head far out her bedroom window, Audrey screamed “Oh my God! Harold, NOOO!”

She ran downstairs and out the front door. Audrey's heart was racing and she could barely catch a breath. Good thing both of their mothers were grocery shopping and their Dads were both at work.

“Are you CRAZY Boychick? Get down from there!”

“Audrey, watch...I'm a bird...I'm a bird...I'm a kamikaze pilot. Watch me fly Audrey.”

“Kamikaze pilots at least had planes, you idiot! Get off the roof Boychick… You'll fall and hurt yourself.”

“I'm ten years old, I know what I'm doing. You sound like my Maaaaaa….”

Audrey gently helped her injured friend out of the thorny bushes. His arms and legs were badly scraped and a protruding piece the storm gutter had ripped a hole in his short sleeve shirt. Boychick was embarrassed by the fall, but thrilled that he had flown.

"Did you see me, Audrey? Did you see me fly? It was great! I'm doing it again."

"You're such a schmuck sometimes Boychick! Only a moron would get back up on that..... Oh my God. Look, here comes the station wagon."

"It's my Mom! She'll kill me if she finds out I was on the roof. Think fast!"

Audrey pushed Boychick into the pricker bushes as hard as she could. He came up crying, ready to knock her stupid block off.

Lynn Silverman nearly hit the mailbox trying to quickly park the station wagon. Tires squealed. Groceries and little sister Ruthie bounced around inside the car.

The entire neighborhood could hear Audrey's voice loud and firm. "That's what you get for calling me a sissy, Boychick Silverman! So what if I play with dolls? GI Joe is a doll too… and you know where you can hide your GI Joe, HAROLD."

"Stay in the car, Ruthie."

Six year old Ruthie stayed in the car as she was told but couldn't resist a jab at her brother. She rolled a back window down and poked out her head and scrawny shoulders, nearly falling out.

“Hey Boychick”… when he looked, she stuck out her tongue and sprayed a long Bronx cheer.

“Enough, Ruthie!”

Lynn appeared to be quite angry. She stepped in front of Audrey as Boychick was threatening to throw a punch. This fight was probably a baloney story, but as long as Audrey was involved Lynn wasn't worried. She'd play along.

“Get in the house and clean up young man. Your Dad will deal with you later. Fight's over.”

“And you Audrey. I'm surprised - a young pretty Jewish girl fighting like a wild animal. Your Mother and I will discuss this over mahjong tonight.”

After his bath, Boychick waited at his bedroom window. Across his yard, in Audrey's bedroom window, he could only see the frilly lamp on her white nightstand.

Finally her window opened and there she was… freshly washed, bright-eyed, ten year old Audrey looking at him, smiling.

She was pleased with herself to have

saved Boychick's young skin today. His mother would have grounded him for at least a week if she knew he was playing Kamikaze Pilot on the roof.

Audrey probably also saved Boychick's tushy from a savage beating by Dave the Pants Man's all-leather belt. The good leather was saved for special occasions such as weddings, bar mitzvahs and beating Harold.

As Boychick looked across at Audrey he wanted to tell her "thank you", or "you're a real friend" or "I love you". Where did that thought come from?

Instead, he waved to get her attention and then flipped her "the bird". He really didn't like girls that much anyway.

Audrey sneered as only a ten year old girl can sneer, and closed her curtains.

THE RED HAND OF DAVE
as told by Langameintza, the Shpeiler

New Jersey, Summer, 1972

Langameintza here...your Shpeiler (storyteller). I'm no mind reader, but I can see trouble coming.

I live in the house next to the Silverman family, at the top of First Avenue hill. Such a beautiful view of suburban north Jersey! Three blocks below is MacArthur Blvd, and the highway to the city.

From my front yard, that hot summer day, I could see the two 11 year old boys horsing around like boys do.

Boychick's cousin Seymour arrived a few days before for the annual month-long visit nicknamed "Camp Silverman".

It was so hot and schvitzy that summer day. With nothing better to do, I was standing in my yard, watching. An old man like me can't just sit in a chair all day long. Okay, I was watching the boys… so sue me.

The way Boychick and Seymour were acting, I knew these two foolish boys would cause some trouble soon… I have that talent.

In Yiddish we say (I'll translate to English), "A fool falls on his back and bruises his nose." They should be so lucky to only bruise a nose.

Seymour was a tall boy, and smart… actually bright and clever describe him better. On his own he was somewhat shy, preferring to watch and listen before joining in.

A good-natured creative friendly boy, this Seymour. He had a knack for telling funny jokes… not that I'm listening.

Okay...awright... It's a hot day and the window's open.

Individually Boychick and Seymour were active self-reliant kids. The problem was keeping them busy. Both tended to get bored easily - and boredom leads directly to trouble.

When the two cousins were together, all shyness disappeared. Both personalities grew confident and boisterous, or as Boychick's mother Lynn termed it, "just-us" independent.

Their games did not include Boychick's six year old sister Ruthie. While the two cousins were busy, Lynn was able to spend quality time with her clever young daughter. They enjoyed days of shopping, swimming, and going out for lunch.

Boychick and Seymour were born only days apart. Rumor had it that Lynn and her sister, who rarely agreed on anything, planned to have children on the same day. As it turned out, Seymour took his time in the womb while Harold was impatient to be born. Harold always kidded his younger cousin to “Mind your elders”.

The two boys clicked the moment they met. Right away Boychick asked, “Do you like The Three Stooges?”

Seymour’s quick response was an attempted two-finger eye gouge, which Boychick easily blocked with an open hand at his forehead.

“You knucklehead!”

“Porcupine!”

That exchange led to the "Niagara Falls" routine. Both boys knew every line and movement.

They were trying to play cowboys and indians, but it was mostly running around the yard.

“I'm tired of being the Indian Boychick. Let's play something else.”

“How about squirt Seymour with the hose? That's a fun game.”

“Boychick, if I had a dog with a face like yours, I'd shave his butt and make him walk backwards.”

Langameintza here. Sorry to intrude on

the shpiel. What did I tell you? This comedian kid Seymour had timing as well as talent. Thirty pounds more he's Buddy Hackett.

So from my window I'm watching two active independent playful boys. No adult supervision. I could see trouble coming.

You should know all this happened years ago when Boychick was eleven. Who knew then from child abuse? When a kid got out of line, his father dealt with it. If the child was willful or dangerous, that kid felt the punishment on his tuchas!

"Funny joke, Seymour. That line is way older than me. I know… Let's chuck rocks."

"Okay. Bet I can hit that Cadillac."

"NOOOO!!! That's Mr. Langa..."

"HEY YOU MASHUGANA! Stay away from mine Cadillac. I teach you to mess with a man's beautiful car!"

"Boychick… Is he always in the window watching us?"

"Almost always, but he's okay."

"What do we do now? I'm bored. Hey I know... there's a number you can dial to test the phone line. Let's see if it works."

Boychick wasn't usually home on the day Jessalyn cleaned the house, but this was summer vacation.

Jessie was much more than a maid to the Silverman family. A tiny rail-thin woman, Jessalynn blessed everyone with her warm heart and her boundless energy.

Her life had been dedicated to her son. With Jessie's approval he joined the military. One week after basic training her son was assigned to a base in Alaska.

When Dave and Lynn's daughter Ruthie was born, undersized and sickly, a neighbor suggested Jessalynn could be a big help with the laundry and cleaning.

Dave Silverman, known as "The Pants Man", agreed. Now six years later, Jessie had become a true friend and part of the Silverman family.

Watching the two cousins was not Jessie's responsibility. Besides, she had a mountain of laundry to fold, and two bathrooms to clean.

The more Jessalynn did her chores and ignored the boys, the more Cousin Seymour wanted to play tricks on her. He dialed the phone number that would ring back to test the line, then hung up and waited.

Rrrrrrrriiiiiiinnnnngggggg

“Silverman residence, Jessalyn speaking. Hello? Hello? No one there.”

The boys started laughing loudly in The Family Room. Jessie wondered why, but preferred to ignore them, returning to the task at hand, folding Dave's BVDs.

Rrrrrrrriiiiiiinnnnngggggg

“Silverman residence. Hello? Hello? Must be a wrong number.”

Again the boys were laughing hysterically. Jessie recalled overhearing Lynn tell her husband that this cousin liked to tell dirty jokes to Boychick.

“That must be why they're laughing like that.” she thought. “Better not to know, or ever ask about boy things.”

Rrrrrrrriiiiiiinnnnngggggg

“What's going on with this phone?! Hello? Silverman residence.”

Three times they had made Jessie drop everything to answer the phone. Both cousins were rolling on the hard tile floor laughing, which hurt elbows and knees. Ever since the Family Room fire, it wasn't safe to have carpet where Boychick played.

“Are you boys doing something with the phone?”

Seymour's shirt was soaked in tears from his own laughter.

“Hello Boychick?...” Seymour mimicked in Jessie’s voice... “Silverman residence. Funny maid speaking.”

He laughed at his Jessie imitation. “What a goofy lady.”

“We better stop Seymour.”

“One more time just for laughs.”

“I don't think you better.”

But the joke was going so well and Boychick had laughed just as loud as his cousin. Now Seymour was unstoppable.

Rrrrrrrriiiiiiinnnnngggggg

“If that's you kids clowning again I'm calling your father at the pants store!”

“Hello...Silverman residence. Jessie speaking. Hello? BOYCHICK!!! SEYMOUR!!! I’LL GET YOU BOYS FOR THIS!”

The boys decided it was time to escape out the back door. By the time Jessie looked outside, Boychick and Seymour were halfway down the block, panting for breath, but still laughing.

“That was mean Seymour. I like Jessie.”

“Did you see her face?”..... (imitating Jessie’s voice) “Silverman residence… No one speaking. Wicked fun!”

“Okay Seymour. Now that you had your kicks, what do we do? I'm still bored.”

“Let's swing your Dad's golf clubs!”

“Okay they're in the garage. Be quiet so Jessalyn doesn't hear us. We can play in the front yard.”

“Boychick… there's that creepy old guy in his window again. HEY OLD MAN… want to eat golf ball?”

"I show you who's going to eat golf ball you little pissers."

"Stop Seymour, Mr. Langameintza is a friend."

"Okay pantywaist. How do you swing a golf club?"

"I'll show you how Dad does it. FORRRRE!"

Langameintza here. Already I tell these boys stay away from mine Cadillac. Then Seymour wants I should eat golf ball.

From my window I could see it coming… trouble. Two wiseguy boys. No parents around to watch. Summer vacation. Oy vay!! I could see this coming.

Boychick's backswing hit Seymour squarely in the cheek, opening up a bloody mess. I should tell you, it was not a bad backswing for a boy his age.

With only a second to think, Boychick ran inside the house and locked the front door. He knew Seymour would get up angry… and Cousin Seymour was much bigger than him.

“You son of a b**** Harold... you hit me on purpose. You son of a b****.”

Through the front door mail slot, Boychick tried to explain his innocence.

“It was an accident, Seymour. I swear! You're my favorite cousin, honest.”

“I believe you, Boychick...Now open the door and let's talk. I'm bleeding real bad.”

“Not until you cool down, Seymour. It was an accident.”

“Accident my ass, you son of a b****. Hit me with a golf club will you? Knock me down like that? I'll show you and your whole family. I'll flood you out like a gopher.”

Seymour wasn't able to strike back directly, so he did what he thought was the next best thing. He turned on the water hose and stuck it through the mail slot in the front door. Running water poured into the front hallway and on into the living room soiling the Silverman's newly installed carpet.

Jessie heard the loud arguing and ran to see if Boychick was okay. By now the living room carpet was totally soaked.

“Oh my god! What have you boys done?!”

“It wasn't me, Jessie. I swear it wasn't me!”

Dripping and flustered, Jessie pushed the water hose back through the mail slot, then went outside and turned off the tap.

Back inside, she vainly attempted to soak up some of the water in the living room by patting the puddles with towels. She was careful not to use any of Dave's beloved linen napkins.

“Get in your room and wait. BOTH OF YOU! I'm calling the pants store.”

Dave hurried home early from work. When he opened his front door, there was a trail of hose water from the front entry through the newly carpeted Living Room. It looked almost like a formerly small creek, swollen from a sudden hard rain.

When Lynn saw the damage to her new Living Room carpet, she could only cry incoherently, mostly because summer vacation had only just begun. Even worse, her nephew Seymour was their guest for three more weeks.

Upstairs in the bedroom, an obviously enraged Dave briefly discussed the incident with his visiting nephew and his son. Boychick couldn't remember ever seeing his father this angry. Judgement was swift.

"Take 'em down, boys ...Both of you."

"But Dad, I didn't..."

"Take 'em down now!!!"

Dave hated this part of being a father, but the boys had been disrespectful to Jessalyn and destructive in his house.

The spanking was deserved. No authorities need be involved. His son, and his nephew, were going to learn to behave.

All of Dave's anger passed through this Hand of Justice, smacking punishment on the rear ends of two young wise guys.

When Dave left the room, the boys felt sore and sorry.

"Owwww. That really hurt. Dad never spanked me like that before."

"Owwww. He barely touched you. Look

what he did to me."

There on Seymour's pale white tuchas, was a huge red hand mark - The Red Hand of Dave.

As sore as Boychick was, he couldn't help but laugh at the large red hand tattoo on cousin Seymour's tushy. He checked, and found out that he also had a huge red hand mark on his tush.

Despite the pain, seeing that same red hand mark on Boychick's tushy started cousin Seymour laughing.

"They're laughing Lynn. I just spanked those boys as hard as I could, and they're laughing. Maybe they need some more."

Dave marched into the boys' room with utmost seriousness.

"Okay boys, what's so funny about a spanking?"

Seymour pulled down his pajama bottoms to show his uncle. There it was… The Red Hand of Dave.

"Move over Boychick", Dave snickered, "this may take awhile."

As Lynn listened to the three of them laughing, she thought about how strange the male of the species can be.

THE TWO-WHEEL BICYCLE

The gift of a big bike was special, but an even better gift was that entire afternoon spent one-on-one with his father.

Harold “Boychick” Silverman was not overly athletic. He had no interest in baseball or basketball. Boychick was more of an "indoor boy". At ten years old, he wasn't muscular or tremendously coordinated, but from imitating his father Boychick managed to show some skill in swimming and golf.

Playing piano came more naturally to him. His fingers displayed exceptional dexterity and emotion, interpreting each piece as if releasing part of his soul into the music.

While his fingers could easily express rhythm, his body was unable to respond. Boychick could not dance. Even his gait walking or running was odd, again from watching and imitating his father.

Some cruel boys at school made remarks about the way Boychick walked, as if his legs stepped first, and then his body caught up. During an outdoor recess period, his unusual running style induced waves of embarrassing laughter from onlooking classmates and even a few teachers.

From the age of ten, Boychick was well aware of his assets and his shortcomings. He prided himself in being proficient at all necessary chores and humbly excelling at every academic challenge.

The daily required trek to elementary school was nearly a straight mile walk in all seasons of weather. Those mile-long walks, day after day since the age of six, gradually improved his leg strength and coordination.

At each intersection along the daily walk to school, fellow students selected as Safety Patrol egotistically (he thought) displayed their angled belt sash and fake badge. They dutifully herded every student at each intersection, making everyone pause for cars.

In first grade Boychick admired the 6th graders chosen for Safety Patrol and he yearned to wear the sash and badge. His occasional outbursts of childish behavior in class were documented by teachers, tarnishing Boychick's chances of ever becoming a Safety Patrol.

At times Boychick seethed with anger at their success while ruminating some self-loathing for his poor choices. It was agonizing to pass them each day at a slow walking pace while other students zoomed past on their big bikes. He wished he had a big 2-wheel bike. He would ride it to school every day.

One day in the late Fall of fourth grade his father surprised him with an amazing present. It wasn't his birthday or his father's birthday. That day wasn't Hanukkah or Christmas or any notable gift-giving holiday. There were times when Boychick's father did noble thoughtful wonderful things simply because he wanted to make his son happy.

That amazing present was a proper 3-speed Royce-Union 2-wheel bicycle. Best of all, his father spent most of that Fall afternoon and early evening patiently teaching him how to ride it.

His father seemed so stern at times, at least that's how the young self-absorbed son viewed his father's facial expressions. Boychick always thought his Dad's intensity was an expectation of perfection - a level of performance impossible for a child to achieve.

Complete explanations about life were not in his father's nature. “The answer my son,“ he would say “is deep within you.”

Boychick was unaware that on these rare occasions when his father's focus was solely on his son, the mature man was trying to be a good parent to his boy on a level of self-expectation he was never sure he could achieve.

On that chilly October 1970 afternoon, the world consisted of only a father, a son and that new Royce-Union 3-speed bicycle.

First attempts to mount the big bike were awkward. It was sized a bit too tall or Boychick's legs were too short. His father, anticipating this possible problem, had brought an adjustable wrench, and expertly lowered the seat.

Together they walked the bike to a high curb. As his father held the bike steady, Boychick used the high curb to place his left foot on the closest pedal and swing his right leg over the center bar.

Success! He was soon riding, with his father running alongside only arm's reach away, steadying the bike.

Then Boychick realized his father had stopped aiding. That was his fatherly nature in all things - allowing his son to find his own way, and fail or succeed in his own way.

Attempt after attempt, his father's patience with his son never wavered. No prompting was ever necessary as Boychick rose from each fall, ignored skinned knees, walked the big bike to the closest curb and tried again. Each try he rode farther and balanced better. He learned to turn smoothly, slow and stop with hand brakes and finally he learned to change gears.

There were no feelings of an expectation level. Both father and son had absolute faith in success. If he mastered this bicycle, Boychick would be allowed to ride it to school, past those Safety Patrol students with their sashes and their badges. How envious they would be!

Several times Boychick saw his Dad's silent nod, meaning they would be briefly interrupted by cars. One car approaching at high speed broke his father's calm veneer, sparking a volcanic outburst of quick temper.

"SLOW DOWN!" he screamed, then quickly gained composure and refocused on the task and its success.

All that Autumn afternoon and into the early evening, a busy father solely dedicated time to teach his young son to ride a big bike. Wordlessly, completely in character, a father showed by his actions how much he truly loved his son.

WORM ZEITZ

Narrated by Langameintza “The Shpeiler”

1 - LASHON HARA

My name is Langameintza The Shpeiler”. I remember much of the goings-on in this north Jersey neighborhood in great detail, but I'm nobody's mavin. My pleasure is relating these memories as interesting and even funny stories. This particular story is interesting, but not so funny. Maybe it will have a happy ending - we will see.

I've known Harold “Boychick” Silverman since he was born... before even. I attended his Bris. I've watched him get taller and smarter. I see him leave for school in the morning and hear him practicing piano every afternoon...not that I'm watching or listening.

My late wife Rhoda and I had no children, so over the years Boychick Silverman has become very special to me. When he is happy, it makes me happy. The rare times anyone has teased or bullied Harold Boychick Silverman it offended me as well. In Yiddish we say (I'll translate) "For your children's sake you would tear the world apart."

By his early teens Harold “Boychick” Silverman enjoyed a large and growing circle of friends, Jewish as well as goyim. Within that circle there were three very special close friends - Mark Zeitz, Marvin Goldstein and Stanley Zuckerman. The four boys started first grade together. Their families all live in this neighborhood and belong to Temple Beth-Shalom.

Being close friends with Mark Zeitz came with a problem - an older brother aptly named Bridke Meisman. In Yiddish the name translates as "horrible monster". This boy was not in Boychick's circle of friends...or anybody's circle.

Bridke Meisman Zeitz had a well-deserved reputation as a rude, foul-mouthed bully. He was larger, older and more muscular than most boys, except

Stanley Zuckerman who was taller. It was impossible to be around Bridke. What to do when your friend has a Dybbuk for a brother?

It is not my nature to commit “lashon hara” - a Hebrew phrase for speaking evil of someone - even if it's true. This is considered a sin in the State of Israel, and not very nice in America.

The Torah instructs us "Do not hate your brother in your heart or bear a grudge against anyone." (Leviticus 19:16). There is always hope that people can change for the better.

Scholars remind us "corn can grow in manure." The truth is, not every garden grows flowers, some grow weeds. In my seventy-plus years I've realized sadly, as there are angels, so also there are devils, bullies and irritants - what we call in Yiddish “vantz” (bedbugs).

A true Shpeiler must tell stories both good and bad. Better I should start from the beginning.

2 - ZEITZ MISHPOCHA

Flossie and her husband Robert Zeitz grew up in Brooklyn. Both families emigrated to America in the 1880s. Her family became. Americanized Reform Jews, blocking all memories of their Russian past. His family remained Orthodox, able to trace their ancestry back to Bohemia in the1400s.

The name Zeitz in Old German refers to the art and science of bee-keeping, an important function in the medieval Jewish community. Honey was determined by scholars to be kosher, even though the bee was not. Zeitz family honey was the main sweetener for generations.

During The Plague, Germany and especially Poland suffered many deaths, leaving estates and farmlands eerily vacant. Most Jews lived in their own shtetyls, apart from the Christians. By dutifully observing kosher laws Jews had little opportunity to contract or spread the disease.

When the Plague subsided, Polish nobles invited Jewish families, like the Zeitz bee-keepers, to live in vacant serf houses and farm the rich soil, without persecution. For hundreds of years, devoutly religious Zeitz men were successful farmers and sold their honey in relative peace.

When Jews were blamed for the murder of Czar Alexander in 1881, Poland was no longer a safe haven. The Zeitz family quietly sold their stocks of honey, their harvested produce and all their animals - enough money to travel to England, then book 3rd class steerage to America.

Growing up in Brooklyn NY, the grandson of immigrants, Robert Zeitz felt privileged to read Torah, Talmud, and even Kabbalah. Religious study imparted valuable Jewish wisdom, but almost no social skills. Robert grew up shy and reserved.

An unfortunate inherited hair-lip complicated life even more. The surgical repair left a noticeable scar. By the age of 16 Robert was able to cover the scar with a thick moustache.

When he was 18, Robert had gained confidence and was lucky enough to meet Flossie, a personable friendly attractive young woman. She possessed all the social skills he lacked. Both families approved the match. After a suitable courtship they were married.

Flossie's new husband taught religious studies, providing financial stability, but he remained socially awkward. She tried to introduce him to culture and friends. He was numb to all efforts.

Eventually Robert agreed to shave his beard and cut his payot (long sideburns), but kept the mustache to cover his hairlip scar. He continued to keep kosher, wore a yarmulke on his head, and a tallit under his shirt.

Flossie’s family embraced American Reform Judaism and ate whatever they liked, even shellfish and pork. They attended holiday services, and memorized Hebrew prayers, but nobody in her family understood Yiddish. Robert's family disapproved of "praying like goyim".

Family opinions and pressure became too much. The young couple decided to start their family in the suburbs. Several Jewish day schools in North Jersey advertised for teachers with Robert's background. Flossie agreed this was a welcome opportunity. In August 1958, before the school year started, they left Brooklyn to settle in a comfortable neighborhood in north Jersey.

3 - MEISKEIT ZEITZ

An unusual baby was born in 1959 at nearby North Jersey Jewish Hospital to parents Robert and Flossie Zeitz. The physical appearance of this child shocked the medical delivery team and also the boy's father. Even the most experienced nurses had never seen such an awkwardly shaped head, no detectable neck and a distinct hairlip.

Flossie Zeitz counted ten fingers, ten toes, and one…well, since the baby was male I'm sure you know, so I don't have to say. A first-time mother, she was relieved to have a healthy boy. Flossie was certain the hereditary Zeitz hair lip and even the oddly shaped head could be fixed. In many ways the child resembled photos she'd seen of Robert's grandfather.

A hospital staffer pasted a comical sticker over the crib ID which read "Mieskeit Zeitz". The kindest translation of "mieskeit" is "not handsome", but in Yiddish such meanings are much more colorful.

The baby's crib ID tag faced the Nurse's entrance, so it could only be seen by the amused hospital staff. Family was never aware why the Pediatric doctors and nurses were all so giddy. This was truly an ugly child. Nurses even joked about lining the crib with hay or straw.

One week later the baby still had no name. Flossie offered several suggestions, but Robert insisted the decision was his.

Both families gathered for a traditional Bris. Mohel Eliyahu Ben-Zion viewed the odd Zeitz baby with some serious concern beyond just facial appearance. The child's tiny gender size required the Mohel to put on his reading glasses to confirm maleness before starting the service. Guests who secretly disliked Robert for years decided that this odd baby was either God's justice, or His sense of humor.

All that week Flossie noticed that her husband seemed more aloof than usual. He seemed perplexed, as if contemplating his own future. A fairly educated man, Robert remained socially awkward, even with his wife. Struggling on a teacher's salary, he had become an irritable miser with few if any friends. Prospective friends always noticed his repaired hair-lip. At his happiest moments the man could not fashion a complete smile.

On the baby's eighth day, Robert named his son Bridke Meisman Zeitz, with the unfortunate initials "BM". Flossie thought the name sounded Old World cultural, maybe even Biblical. During the circumcision, the Mohel volunteered a Hebrew name "Dybbuk". Robert heartily agreed.

As the Bris service concluded, while guests were still sipping strong coffee and enjoying deli sandwiches, Robert Zeitz quietly packed his clothes. With an arm full of books and the recurring mental picture of his mieskeit baby, Robert exited through the back door, hailed a cab then boarded a bus back to Brooklyn.

Flossie didn't miss her husband or the stress of his Orthodox lifestyle. She pushed their mandatory separate beds together to make one King size, poured herself two fingers of straight Scotch, lit a cigarette and happily listened to rock'n'roll on her radio.

Several years later, a woman at Temple told Flossie that her son's name, “Bridke Meisman”, was Yiddish for “horrible monster”. She regretted allowing Robert to name her child but it was accurate. The Hebrew name given by the Mohel, “Dybbuk”, translated as "an evil entity who steals souls". That, she thought, remained to be seen.

Robert Zeitz often regretted leaving his dear wife. Two years later his Brooklyn family urged him to return to New Jersey and try again. The reunion lasted less than a week and nearly cost the man his sanity. Robert loved Flossie but could not cope with that monster child. They agreed to separate but never divorce.

One positive result of the short tryst was the creation of their second son Mark - a normal healthy child, who became Boychick's close friend.

4 - A FITTING NICKNAME

In early childhood, Bridke often screamed for attention. The only way to quiet him was with candy or ice cream. The more the boy misbehaved, the more candy and ice cream were required to shut him up. At rare times Bridke displayed the polite behavior of a normal child. It was expected so it was ignored, which confused the child.

Evil behavior and loud tantrums always gained him attention and sweets. The boy reasoned that all he had to do for rewards was to cruelly embarrass his mother or anyone they met in the grocery store, the bank or even at Temple. Flossie always had a lollipop or candy bar in her purse.

By the age of ten, mere tantrums for candy no longer fulfilled Bridke's appetite. He was forbidden to tease his younger brother. Instead, he satisfied himself by insulting and bullying selected innocent victims.

Like a bloodthirsty vampire, "BM" poked his target with continuous verbal prodding to create an emotional incision. Once a wound was open he would chaff and poke and probe and frustrate until the victim became unhinged.

His most powerful weapon was deeply stabbing personal insults that many would remember word for word long into the future.

Anyone and everyone BM Zeitz met, eventually despised him. Even the kindest and most forgiving good souls found themselves walking away completely shaken by the experience. Abusing innocents fed his evil soul. It nourished and sustained him. This is the nature of a true Dybbuk.

Flossie began to blame herself for such a son. The School Counselor was consulted. That seasoned professional confirmed that Flossie was a kind caring mother, and in no way responsible for her son's bad behavior. He explained Bridke's personality issues as an attempt at social adjustment. The boy was just relieving built-up anxiety.

Nose-to-nose, Flossie informed The School Counselor that she had shopped Hebrew National for years, so she recognized baloney.

Bridke inherited the Zeitz hair lip, but actually enjoyed the special attention and pity. Flossie insisted it be fixed. The surgery pulled tiny facial muscles into an odd expression which repulsed nearly every childhood playmate and later every sober girl.

To make matters worse, while attempting to play a trumpet, the stitched area reopened, creating a larger permanent scar.

By the age of fifteen Bridke grew a thick moustache (like his father) to cover the disfigurement. With renewed confidence from the moustache, he asked to be enrolled at Summer Camp. Flossie happily agreed.

At Camp, Bridke slowly began to socialize with boys his age and a few girls. He was never well liked, but he was not despised.

After a group swim, Bridke's soaked swim trunks fell to his ankles in front of the entire camp. He had some difficulty pulling up the wet trunks, creating much attention. Amused girls at Camp tagged him "Worm". The nickname matched reality in several ways and so it became permanent.

What a strange boy, this Worm - never at ease around people. Anyone trying to be friendly to him felt equally uncomfortable. Even dogs didn't much like him.

He attended high school like other kids his age, and knew how to speak properly, but never seemed to know what to say. Words came out in frustrated short phrases, making him irritable. In a group, his miserable mood spread like cholera.

The only true joy in Worm Zeitz's life was what the boys call "busting balls", like that popular TV show about Brooklyn schoolboys. On the show bigger boys would "rank" that funny Arnold kid, but their TV insults about "Mellow Rolls" were creative and funny. Nobody got hurt. Everyone knew when to stop. Worm Zeitz' insults were cruel and he never cared to stop.

Worm would pick out the weakest of the group, then launch personal insults. When his target clearly had enough abuse, he would gleefully double the quantity and intensity of insults, each followed by an awful high-pitched cackle.

The boy was relentless in his verbal torture, like the guards must have been at Treblinka. If Worm's verbal attack caused a breakdown or real tears, he would show no mercy, continuing for hours with obvious pleasure.

His younger brother Mark was somehow exempt, but caught in the middle. Mark Zeitz couldn't abandon or ignore his older brother. He couldn't defend him or be seen with him either. With much patience and effort, Mark and Bridke managed an uneasy peace.

There was a rumor that Flossie and her ex-husband Robert made a bargain with their son Bridke (Worm) to treat his brother with respect. Otherwise, they believed a wild dog like him should be spayed or neutered.

Busy boys had places to be and busy mothers willing to drive them. Mark's mother, Flossie Zeitz, and Boychick's mother, Lynn worked well together and enjoyed each other's company.

These ladies were doers, actively volunteering whenever needed, and the Temple noticed. Flossie was asked to arrange a carpool rotation with the other mothers. Lynn was asked to organize the Oneg Shabbat (desserts and coffee) following the Friday night Shabbat services.

Flossie made friends easily. She suggested the ladies have a night of their own so Wednesday became MahJong Night. Each week a different lady hosted a lively game and served snacks. Flossie and Boychick's mother Lynn were "regular" players each week. Two or more ladies would play when they could, to serve snacks, charge up the conversation and sit in for bathroom breaks,

Audrey Rosen's mother joined the game for a few months, but she was an aggressive player, often winning $5 or more and gloating afterward. One Wednesday night she served shrimp and has not been invited back.

My Rhoda would have loved playing MahJong with neighbor ladies. If only she hadn't choked to death on a wonton at Madame Chin's. That night we should've gone for pizza.

Worm Zeitz was often a subject of conversation at the Wednesday night MahJong game. These ladies had all heard gossip about the outrageous rude behavior of Flossie's older boy. They felt rachmunas for their friend to have such a son. Some ladies asked many personal questions until Lynn would direct attention back to the mahjong game.

"One Bam....to you Flossie"

"Two Crack."

"Go ahead. Slide some tiles."

Nobody blamed Flossie. She was an outgoing, smart, sociable, nurturing mother who tried her best to improve both sons. Her friendly, polite younger son, Mark, was proof of Flossie's fine mothering skills.

The older boy Bridke refused to study Hebrew or be involved at Temple, mostly due to social issues with the other children. When Mark was bar mitzvahed, it was considered the Temple's finest event ever (until three weeks later when Boychick Silverman was Bar Mitzvah'd).

After many frustrating years of coping with Worm's abusive behavior, Flossie now merely tolerated him. Other family members preferred a phone conversation rather than be in the same room with him.

"Worm" was a trouble-maker but he wasn't stupid. He never started issues with boys larger than him. Worm Zeitz did not like pain or losing. He selected victims who were undersized, not very athletic, and vulnerable - someone who would be easily wounded by simple crude insults. He often eyed Mark's group of close friends, plotting, planning, looking for a victim.

At first he considered insulting Marvin Goldstein, but decided that Marvin was too clever to become sufficiently upset. Also Marvin had loyal friends to defend him, and if necessary, had the speed to run away quickly from a fist fight.

Next, Worm considered insulting Stanley Zuckerman, but a tall athletic confident boy like Stanley might fight back. The bully needed someone smaller, more vulnerable, easily hurt by personal insults. Boychick Silverman was the perfect target.

A dark plan was taking shape in Worm's mind. Once "the game" began, he sensed that Boychick would shrink with fear... memorizing each syllable of the onslaught, taking every jab personally. Worm could already visualize Boychick deteriorating into an emotional outburst - maybe even a flood of real tears.

Worm grinned as he thought to himself, "This will be fun."

5 - MY PRECIOUS

Every weekday morning the school bus picked up students who lived more than a mile away, and returned them in the afternoon. Boychick lived 0.9 miles from the school, so he had to walk or ride a bike.

In first, second and third grades Boychick walked to school every day, At each busy intersection along the route, honor students appointed as Safety Patrol stopped traffic, making sure each child crossed safely.

Harold "Boychick" Silverman detested those phony soapbox student traffic guards with their white strap belt across their chest and their fake tin badge. In truth he was envious. Safety Patrol was an honorary position - a reward for good grades and good behavior. Boychick had ruined his chances with immature behavior.

In October of fourth grade, Boychick's father - known as "Dave the Pants Man" - brought home a wonderful unexpected present - a 26" 3-speed Royce-Union bicycle. Together they spent that afternoon and into the evening learning how to ride it. Boychick treasured his new bicycle. Every night he securely chain-locked it outside the garage.

For one month Boychick rode his bike to school every day, smiling and enjoying the ride. If an intersection was clear, he would whizz past those Safety Patrol boys, sometimes making comments or waving bye-bye.

One November morning the bike was gone. The chain had been cut. His precious bike had been stolen, with no reasons and no clues.

"Who dislikes me? Nobody steals bikes in this neighborhood." he thought to himself. As he sadly walked the familiar 0.9 mile to school, Boychick regretted being mean to those student crossing guards.

"Where's your bike, Bigshot?"

"My bike was stolen. Let me know if you see it."

"Sure thing Mr. Boychick Silverman… 'cause we're such good friends, right? Have you asked Mark Zeitz's brother Worm?"

"It must have been Worm!" Boychick thought to himself. "How can I get my bike back from such a large tough bully?"

Langameintza here, and you should pardon the interruption. That afternoon I was getting some sun on my front porch, minding my own business as the children arrived home from school. Alright alright I was watching the young people...so sue me. I thought it was strange that Boychick walked home, but I just waved hello and didn't ask.

That big mean Zeitz boy - Mark's older brother - was waiting in front of the Silverman house laughing in his high pitch cackle noise. Something metal was in his hands that looked like bicycle handlebars.

"Lose something, pantywaist?" Worm was so pleased with himself he laughed his evil-sounding cackling noise over and over.

"I want my bike back… And don't call me pantywaist."

"You gonna cry meydl beibi? Gonna cry?"

Worm had learned some useful Yiddish words from visiting his Zeitz grandparents in New York. Boychick had just been called a baby girl. Insults in Yiddish were somehow more descriptive and stung worse, so Boychick tried his best to sound tough.

"WORM! You thief. You stole my bike. I want it back!" As soon as he said those words Boychick thought acting tough might have been a bad idea. Worm leaned in closer, waving the handlebars and sneering horribly.

"Tough guy? Boychick tough guy? Now you gotta fight me for the bike.
Tomorrow four o'clock at the Big Field….
Don't be late."

Boychick looked visibly shaken. He shouldn't have reacted, but he wasn't a pantywaist or a baby girl. Now he was scared. He had never been in a fight.

Bridke's insults echoed over and over in his mind.

The confrontation could have been worse. Bridke Zeitz was loud and threatening, but Boychick sensed the bully wasn't violent. The name-calling was just bluster - for Bridke, an amusing game.

It was obvious now that Bridke stole his precious bike and that it would be returned once Bridke's game was done, even if Boychick had to fight to get it back.

Bridke once again laughed that horrible cackling laugh, threw the handlebars in Boychick's yard, then walked away.

6 - THE FIGHT SUBSTITUTION

Bridke "Worm" Zeitz had no social abilities, and no idea of how to attract friends. Instead he became a predator.

Rumors claimed that Bridke had beaten and bloodied several boys but there was no proof. In truth he was a verbal bully, hurling vile insults, emotionally destroying every boy he chose to attack... except one. The exception was a new neighborhood boy named Eric.

Eric was a nice-enough kid, somewhat shy, not Jewish and not at all athletic. He was Boychick's age and size. Nobody knew Eric well. He mostly kept to himself.

The first week of school, Bridke stalked Eric as a perfect target and approached menacingly. Eric assumed this large boy wanted to make friends, so he reached into his pocket and offered a Hershey bar. That offer of chocolate stunned and calmed Bridke. The predator lost all interest in the hunt. Since that day Bridke allowed Eric to follow at a safe distance, much like a Pilot Fish or Remora accompanying a shark.

It occured to Boychick that Eric might be the key to solving this problem. A plan was taking shape. After dinner, Boychick, Marvin, Stanley and Mark met in Marvin's Treehouse. Mark Zeitz kept silent but nodded often. They all agreed that Boychick must arrive totally confident, set out certain rules, then be immediately aggressive. If the plan failed, he should duck and run.

Langameintza your Shpeiler here. Such a nice sunny afternoon outside. Enough television and four white walls already. The kids are just getting home from school. Very curious that once again Boychick walked home. His bike must have a flat tire.

First thing, Boychick dutifully warmed up the Silverman piano with scales and arpeggios. Today's project was The Moonlight Sonata. If Beethovan heard he might have been pleased…, but the man was deaf.

I've known Harold "Boychick" Silverman since he was born - before even. I attended his bris - lovely affair with quality New York bagels and real whitefish. The point is I know this boy. He's not overly athletic. He can be mischievous, but he's a good boy and pals around with nice boys his age. Most of Boychick's friends are also good boys from his public school classes and his Sunday Confirmation classes at Temple Beth-Shalom.

The usual characters that come around are Flossie Zeitz's younger son Mark, that tall athletic kid Stanley Zuckerman, and Boychick's clever best friend Marvin Goldstein. Most days the boys play ball in The Big Field or hang out in Marvin's tree house...not that I'm looking.

When the piano went quiet I stepped outside for air. Why not? What else does an old man have to do but watch TV and count my toes...again. I'm standing in front of my house, minding my own business like always, when I see the boys gather around Boychick next door at the Silverman house. They walked him to The Big Field like soldiers guarding a prisoner.

Two boys were at the field waiting. One was a new neighborhood boy, the same size as Boychick. His family bought the Goldstein house two streets over. The larger boy was Mark Zeitz's older brother, Bridke - the bully they call "Worm" - a mieskeit, noisy, heavy kid with no neck and a scarred upper lip. He was holding most of Boychick's bicycle.

As soon as I saw that Worm kid I could sense trouble coming. I have that talent. It wasn't long until I just happened to witness the fight. Okay...all right..., I was watching the young people, so sue me.

Worm Zeitz advanced toward Boychick with a menacing expression and hairy fists tightly clenched. Stanley and Marvin bravely blocked the bully's approach. Mark Zeitz stood at a respectable distance marking out the fight stage boundaries.

"Tough guy? Boychick tough guy? Fight for your bike."

"Bridke...this isn't a fair fight. We both know you're gonna win easily."

The bully nodded yes, then caught himself smiling and resumed his menacing sneer. The game was not starting as planned. His prey seemed calm. Bridke was confused and a bit curious.

Boychick continued, "I'm not athletic. I've never been in a fight."

He knew he must outwit the bully or deal with certain pain. Boychick decided to use a "Logic Tact" that he learned from one week in Debate Club. Distract and confuse,..alter the advantage,...gain control. He looked straight at the bully and continued his logic.

"I admit that I'm not a very challenging match for a fight. Beating me would be nothing to brag about."

Once again Bridke nodded agreement. It was obvious the confused bully's intensity had lessened. Worm quickly revived into obvious anger. He came to play his evil hunting game, but the prey was not cooperating.

"Enough stall! Start the fight...OR I WILL!"

"Okay Bridke...I'll fight since I've been challenged, but I suggest 'a substitution'. My opponent should be of equal size.... perhaps your new friend Eric.

The bully is out of patience and outwitted. Worm accepts the challenge and pushes the surprised tag-along into the fight area. Boychick's reluctant opponent - 'the substitution' - wants to run away, but can't.

Marvin rings a bell to start the fight. Within seconds Boychick raises his fists, briefly dances around like Muhammed Ali, then lands a hard punch to Eric's chin, knocking the boy down in pain.

"Fight's over." Marvin says. With Mark and Stanley guarding, they quickly lead Boychick (and his bike) away.

BOYCHICK'S BAR MITZVAH

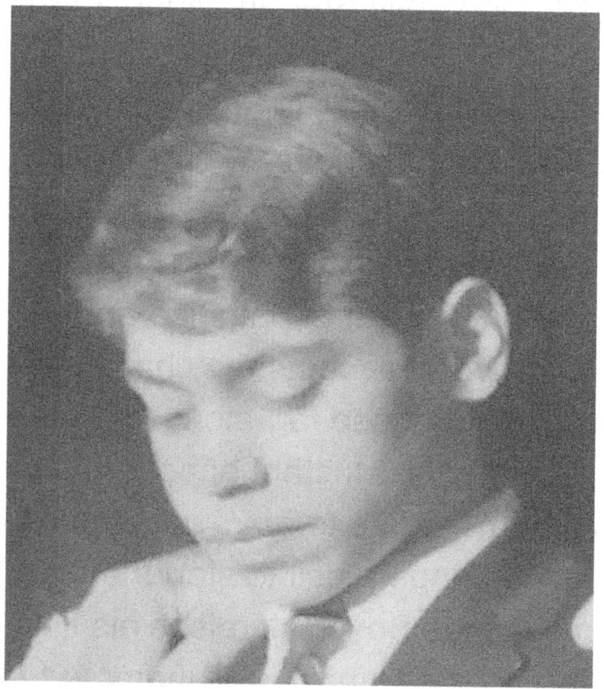

Part 1 - Three Disasters

Harold “Boychick” Silverman's Bar Mitzvah was Lynn Silverman's headache. From the day she confirmed the Bar Mitzvah date, this celebration of manhood, this wonderful event, was a logistical and financial nightmare.

Harold needs books... Harold needs a ride... The photographer wants his deposit... The temple isn't sure the caterer is kosher... The band has another engagement that same night... The florist is allergic to marigolds.... Aunt Sadie can't make it.

Even though this was her first large family party since her wedding, Lynn capably met and solved all the usual problems. Then, she faced the unusual - three major disasters. As we say in Yiddish (I'll translate) "Trouble doesn't come alone".

The first disaster happened eight weeks before the Bar Mitzvah date. It resulted mainly from sticker shock The fearful reaction one gets from the cost of a First-Class Bar Mitzvah is similar to the nauseous reaction some people experience from seeing the price of a fancy new car.

Boychick's father David Silverman, known as "The Pants Man", returned from an exhausting frustrating day at Mr. Shapiro's clothing store, to find receipts totaling more than $6,000, a sum equal to several months of commissions.

For the last few months Dave had remained outwardly patient as he watched this religious rite of passing degenerate into an out-of-control circus. It was taking a toll on his wife, his family and now on him.

Weeks of built-up frustration finally came to a head. Dave became absolutely livid. His eyes bulged and his face flushed red. Drying off his sweat with a clean cloth napkin, he tried again to restrain himself but couldn't.

"Lynn... call "The Bar Mitzvah Factory"! This dog-and-pony show you call a Bar Mitzvah is now cancelled. Do you hear me? CANCELLED!!! I gave you a budget to work with. Was I talking to myself? The boy can read his Torah portion in the small Chapel with ten relatives. Believe me, God will understand."

Harold stepped between his parents to answer his father before Lynn had a chance to dry her tears. He knew his father had a good heart.

"Dad, this is the most important event in my life. Don't ruin it for me."

The boy turned away briefly to wipe his eyes and regain his composure.

"Mom's done her best to make this a nice party and she's done all the schlepping. If it costs too much, I'll wash cars or get a job. Please don't cancel my Bar Mitzvah."

Boychick looked down at his feet. He appeared to be sobbing.

Dave had heard enough. He broke down seeing his sad-eyed son pleading this way.

"We'll manage son. I had a tough day today. Of course we won't cancel your Bar Mitzvah."

Lynn winked at her son - the same expressive knowing wink as her father, Grandpa Ben. She was not at all fooled by Boychick's pretense of sincerity. She knew that her son had put one over on old Dad.

The second disaster occurred six weeks before the scheduled Bar Mitzvah date. A skillet of french-fry oil boiling in a pan on the stove, caught fire. Boychick was first on the scene.

Thinking quickly, he tried to douse the flames with a large pan of water. Intense smoke filled the kitchen then the entire house, coating every wall and ceiling with black soot.

It had been nine years since Boychick's chemistry set burned the dining room table. Two years later, while Boychick was playing with cigarettes, a lit match ignited the Family Room carpet and drapes. The insurance company paid for damages then cancelled the family's homeowners insurance.

Their agent and good friend Uncle Max

was sympathetic, but very wary of insuring Dave's house ever again. Somehow he had been persuaded that Boychick was older now, and more responsible..

"What could happen, Max? The kid is a mature teenager."

Against his better judgement Max okayed the policy. Two weeks later, Uncle Max once again helped to file the claim for fire and smoke damage.

The insurance settlement paid for painting the entire house and steam-cleaning all their rugs and upholstery. Painters finished only three days before the first out-of-towners arrived.

The third disaster happened four weeks before the Bar Mitzvah, on the Temple's sloping driveway.

Lynn Silverman had just dropped off her son and his friends for Hebrew school. She was chatting with Flossie Zeitz about Bar Mitzvah invitations, decent caterers and proper seating arrangements.

Somehow Lynn had left the station wagon in Neutral instead of Park. The heavy vehicle rolled gradually backwards down the driveway slope and over her ankle, making a loud cracking noise.

Flossie thought quickly. She drove her badly injured friend to the hospital, rather than have the sound of an ambulance disturb the boys' Hebrew class.

Weeks later on Boychick's big day, relatives hardly noticed Lynn's limp, but many commented on her beautiful floor-length gown.

BOYCHICK'S BAR MITZVAH

Part 2 - The Rite Of Manhood

If you're wondering... the answer is yes. I, Langamintza, was an invited guest at Boychick's Bar Mitzvah. Why not? I've lived next door since before the boy was born.

To some, a Bar Mitzvah is just food, conversation and dancing, Reform Jews especially get caught up in impressing somebody with a show of fine clothes, fancy jewelry, loud music and lavish expense. They forget the real reason a boy is asked to perform this ancient ritual of Bar Mitzvah. They forget it is about gathering family to acknowledge the new generation. They forget Bar Mitzvah is about passing the Torah from father to son.

The service went beautifully. Rabbi Shlubowitz chanted the traditional blessings before opening the Ark which contained all five of the Temple's decorated Torahs.

With practiced care, the Rabbi respectfully lifted the small center Torah used for services, carried it to the pulpit, removed its ornate cover and medallions, then called father David Silverman and son Harold

Silverman to the podium.

The Bar Mitzvah boy stood onstage at the podium with his proud father next to him, looking out at all his relatives and friends. Harold gestured to the congregation to rise for the blessings before reading from the Torah. My heart was so full to hear Harold lead the Hebrew prayers.

"Baruch atah adonai…" Harold chanted.

In unison the congregation responded, "Baruch atah adonai l'elolom voed."

Harold continued in a confident voice.

"Baruch atah adonai, eloheynu melech ha'olam. Asher notan lanu et torahto. Baruch atah adonai, notan hatorah. Amen."

Then Harold "Boychick" Silverman chanted from the Book of Moses - the sacred Torah - in perfect Hebrew. This special boy that I've known since he was born, became a man before my very eyes. If I was his own father I, Langameintza, could not have been prouder.

He performed his Torah portion expertly, chanted the closing blessing, then seated everyone at the proper time. Relatives claimed that the spirit of Ed Sullivan was reborn in Harold Silverman he was such a showman. At that thought Mr. Sullivan's corpse rotated twice.

Noisy cheering broke out in the front row after Harold finished his Torah portion. Rabbi Shlubowitz was called on to restore order.

His best friends Zeitz, Zuckerman and Marvin Goldstein studied with Harold hour after hour, day after day to learn the difficult Hebrew prayers and Torah portions.

When Harold finished his Torah portion and prayers without a mistake the boys instinctively stood up shouting, slapping "high fives" and cheering for their friend.

"That-a-boy, Boychick!" Marvin Goldstein yelled, jumping over Zuckerman to slap more high fives with Zeitz. All three boys flashed a "thumbs up" with big proud smiles on their faces.

Rabbi Shlubowitz appeared quite ruffled and unamused by the loud interruption. As he lifted his reading glasses he noticed Boychick's palm in the air, waiting for the Rabbi's response. The congregation was hushed… expecting the worst.

"Ah, vat de hell," the old Rabbi remarked, and slapped Harold a high five. "Goot chob Boychick."

BOYCHICK'S BAR MITZVAH

Part 3 - Only The Best For My Boy

Boychick's Bar Mitzvah suit displayed the latest in fashion. His father, Dave, known as "The Pants Man", had sent to Europe for the fabric and to the Far East for the buttons. Every stitch was hand-sewn exactly as it appeared in the Bamberger catalog.

"Only the best for my boy" Dave often remarked.

Guests dined on Chicken Kiev, danced to live band music, and wandered from table to table greeting old friends and schmoozing with each other.

My little white seating card was marked "Langameintza - 7." At table seven I met Lynn's cousin Sheldon, his wife Elaine, and some of Grandma Esther's mishpocha. We mostly discussed the old days in Brooklyn, different ways to make kreplach, and the slow death of Yiddish as a spoken language.

Esther's mishpocha were a delight to spend time with. Their stories kept me occupied from the salad to the dessert. Attempts at intelligent conversation with Lynn's cousin Sheldon was quite another matter.

Everyone in both Lynn and Dave's families knew that Sheldon was useless. He managed to marry, but never worked. Some maintained he was just a slow learner, or possibly lacked oxygen at birth. Short and stocky with a nondescript face, Sheldon had never found his calling. The truth is he was useless.

Grandma Esther was such a truly sweet polite woman. She always had a way of being truthful without insulting or hurting someone's feelings. When asked, she brilliantly described Sheldon as “too light for heavy work and too heavy for light work.”

The invited guests lit their cigarettes with “Boychick” matches, snacked on “Boychick” chocolates and wiped their faces with “Boychick” napkins. Lynn had left no stone unturned in providing the best Bar Mitzvah any boy ever had. It was certainly better than what Flossie Zeitz had for her son Mark.

The band played “Trieste” with a bossa-nova beat, then modulated to “Wave”. Everyone had a good laugh at the sight of portly Grandpa Ben dancing with Boychick's pathetically skinny, pale nine year old sister Ruthie.

"Grandpa, you're holding me too tight", Ruthie whined.

Dave gently tapped his son, the Bar Mitzvah boy, on his shoulder.

"Dance with your mother Boychick." his father whispered, "Your grandfather and I will meet you outside in 15 minutes".

"What's up Grandpa?" Boychick shivered from the freezing New Jersey winter wind. He hadn't thought to grab a coat.

"Your father and I rented this limo for your Bar Mitzvah present. Quickly Boychick, get in where it's warm."

Boychick gazed in amazement at the stretch black Cadillac limousine parked in the street behind Temple Beth-Shalom. Dave tried to hide the prankish smile on his face, a look that Boychick had never seen.

Something odd was going on. As always Grandpa Ben spoke only with his bright, clear, loving eyes. Their trust was absolute, no words were needed.

"What the hell," Boychick thought to himself. "It's too cold to stay outside."

"That's the boy."

Grandpa and Dave returned to the party so as not to arouse the ladies' suspicion. They all danced a family Hora in honor of the new Bar Mitzvah.

Oh Elohim! was Boychick glad he was so curious. Inside the darkened stretch limo, lying on the spacious leather-upholstered back seat, was the most gorgeous blue-eyed mature blonde woman Boychick had ever seen. Her body was wrapped in black fur and she had drenched herself in Chanel No.5.

As the curva's knowledgeable hands reached to unzip Boychick's new hand-sewn Bar Mitzvah pants, her ample ivory breasts spilled out of the fur.

"Happy Bar Mitzvah, Boychick", she purred.

No one noticed Boychick's return. It was as if he had only gone to the restroom.

"Did you wash your hands Harold?" his mother asked.

"Yes. MOTHER."

"Don't be such a smart-alec Boychick... and wipe that silly smirk off your face, it's time for your speech."

The speech to his family was short. It had to be... Boychick couldn't stop laughing. Proud father Dave couldn't stop laughing either - he was totally in tears, unable to compose himself.

None of the ladies understood the commotion. They assumed Boychick had been allowed a drink or two. Silly men and their rituals of manhood!

An interesting aside - Harold's given Hebrew name at birth was "Avram", the name biblical Abraham was called before he discovered God and became a complete man. For young Harold the name contained no significance until this exact minute.

Grandpa Ben regained his composure. He borrowed the band's microphone to introduce the Bar Mitzvah boy to his family.

"Ladies and gentlemen, I present to you my grandson, Harold **Abraham** Silverman."

Family and friends in unison yelled "Mazel tov!"

"Today,..." Boychick snickered, watching the huge teary smile on his Dad's face, "Today I am a man."

THE BATTLE OF SILVERMAN'S PIANO

Langameintza the Shpeiler here. Every afternoon after school The Battle of Silverman's Piano raged, loud enough to echo down First Avenue Hill. From my house next door I could hear it all clearly.

First his mother Lynn would start with 'practice practice", answered by Boychick with the excuses and the whining. Between the complaining was sometimes some fine piano playing - nothing that would open at Carnegie Hall mind you, but superb quality for this part of General MacArthur Boulevard.

"God, Mom. Do I have to practice right now? The weather's so nice… I should be outside."

"Boychick. Piano is something we want for you. You agreed to practice. You'll thank me when you're older."

"But why can't I do this later? Pleeeese! The piano will still be here tonight."

"You're starting again. Every day the same. Make some music. Eyes forward. Fingers on the keys. Play!"

Lynn knew Boychick would focus for only a short while. Her son clearly had musical talent and a natural feel for the piano, but he lacked self-discipline.

Before he was born she would sit in the family room next to the record player, playing classical music with her large belly close to the speaker. The boy was born with a love of music but not much patience. She made him practice as much as humanly possible. In a short time she would lose this battle.

"Mom... thirty minutes is plenty of practice. The guys are playing touch football in the Big Field. Pleeeease!"

"Play me your Bach Invention again then go already. You whine worse than your little sister Ruthie."

Another day, another con job, though conning Mom was a hollow victory. Boychick knew deep down that Lynn was totally wise to his every scheme.

He could turn a story upside-down in the most convenient way. He could swear that snowflakes were blue or the President of the United States was coming to dinner. Mom would dutifully nod her agreement with great sincerity, but she could not be fooled. She always knew. Lynn's great strength was she never admitted she knew. A schemer would get what he deserved... and Boychick Silverman was a schemer. Was he EVER!

TOUCH FOOTBALL

Jewish boys played touch football, even asthmatic Jewish boys like Boychick. The goyim could bash each others' heads and break bones playing tackle. Jewish boys played for the strategy of the game… and the exercise… and the friendship… and the side-bets.

"Here's the plan. My best friend Marvin Goldstein will toss with everyone before the game, He's the most athletic and a real schmoozer. After the toss he'll tell us who's on today and who's not. Then we'll set some odds and take bets from both sides. We'll clean up!"

The first game Boychick and his friends did clean up – eighty-five dollars. Everyone involved got paid. Every boy was happy. Marvin bought the Sony Walkman he wanted. Boychick was a hero. "Boychick the Greek" they teased.

The next afternoon the other boys hatched their own plan. Stanley Zuckerman, the quarterback for the "shirts" team made a deal with Mark Zeitz, Both teams would double the bet then throw the game.

Marvin came by to toss and schmooze,

this time with a new Walkman clipped to his waist. Stanley fielded a hard throw, then pretended the awkward catch jammed his middle finger. He held the finger tenderly and winced in imaginary pain.

"Dammit, my right hand, too. I owe that Zeitz one after yesterday. With nine fingers I'll still beat his ass."

Marvin practically ran to his best friend Boychick, nearly tripping on his dangling ear phone wires.

"Zuckerman's hurt. Zeitz is a sure thing. They still want to double the bet."

Boychick was a little worried, but his overconfidence after yesterday's big win overcame most doubts. Still there was a risk the scheme may not work as well a 2nd time.

"Marvin, give me a minute to think."

It seemed to Marvin that his friend was truly unsure what to do. Boychick walked a few steps, then sat himself on a patch of grass. He closed his eyes and considered his options.

Whenever he was outside, Boychick thought of Audrey Rosen... the soft curls of her shoulder-length auburn hair waving in the breeze as she ran across the Big Field to him.

Her small firm pointed boobs slightly

bobbed up and down under the thin fabric of her halter-top as she approached. The new gold bracelet, bought for her as a gift from today's winnings, glistened in the bright sunshine. Her soft breathy voice and full lips called to him.

"Oh thank you Boychick, thank you! The bracelet is soooo BEAUTIFUL! I'm going to be sooooooo nice to you."

"Marvin...I'll do it! Take the bet. What the hell. If they want to give us their money, who are we to turn it down?"

Marvin untangled the hanging earphone wires of his Walkman and fitted its plugs back in his ears. He smiled happily at the music and at his friend's decision. Being best friends with Boychick Silverman was starting to really pay off.

The rematch of Shirts vs. Skins touch-football began. For most of the first half Boychick exuded confidence. Zeitz's Skins offense sharply executed their plays, marching down the Big Field for several scores. Their defense looked equally strong, holding back the Shirts' offense, forcing them to punt. Boychick's touch football scheme sequel was about to profit $170.

Zuckerman's bomb pass for a

touchdown at the end of the first half must have been a fluke, so Boychick still wasn't worried. If the final score was close, the worst he could do was break even on the bets. Boychick wasn't sure how it was possible, but he actually respected Zuckerman for accurately throwing that far with a painful jammed finger.

The second half was all Shirts. Play after play, touchdown after touchdown Zuckerman threw brilliantly.

He had some skills and once hoped to quarterback the school's varsity football team. Defensive linemen pounded him into reality. The try-out was unsuccessful.

Stanley nearly made the Intramural team, losing that opportunity to a large red-headed, pimple-faced Freshman.

Even in gym class pick-up games, Zuckerman was never picked higher than sixth, but among just Jewish boys Stanley Zuckerman was a star athlete. Now Stanley was leading his Shirts team to a surprising upset victory.

Langameintza here, and you should pardon the interruption. I was not at their Big Field. An old man doesn't involve himself with boys' games, but I heard about it later. The whole neighborhood heard.

If I had been there, I might have imparted some Yiddish wisdom. (I'll translate the phrase to English) "A trick is only clever once."

Beads of sweat built up on Boychick's forehead as the game came to a close. He nervously counted the eighty-one dollars he had in his pocket. It was nowhere near enough to cover the bet.

Marvin had gone to pee after the third touchdown and hadn't come back. Where was he? Boychick refused to believe Marvin turned coward at the worst possible moment. If true, some best friend he was.

"What am I gonna do?" Boychick thought to himself, adding "they'll kill me." He certainly didn't like losing a game or a bet, but worse was the obnoxious way Stanley Zuckerman loudly celebrated his victories.

"Game's over Boychick," Zuckerman laughed. "Pay up!"

"Yeah HAROLD" the other Shirts teammates – and Zietz - chimed in. "We want our MONEY."

Mark Zeitz always sneered when he spoke. His surgically repaired harelip made today's expression a look of evil delight.

Boychick could see that his own quarterback was in on the scam. He now faced an angry mob that knew he couldn't cover the bet. Out-scammed and alone, Boychick was scared. Where was Marvin?

"I...I...I don't have all the money right now. How 'bout if we all meet here tomorrow?"

Zeitz, Zuckerman and the entire Shirts team were closing in on Boychick, all pressing for their winnings. The atmosphere was tense.

Something touched Boychick's hands behind his back, It felt like money, but it couldn't be money. He grasped what was behind him carefully and brought it around to the front. Five twenty-dollar bills! MARVIN!

"One at a time boys. Boychick Silverman always pays his debts."

Thanks to Marvin he once again had complete control.

'Sometimes I win, sometimes I lose, but I always settle everything on the spot. My best friend Marvin here will tell you."

Boychick gave Marvin an unseen squeeze and a very grateful wink.

"I owe you one partner."

THE TREEHOUSE

In seventh grade, Harold “Boychick” Silverman's best friend, Marvin Goldstein, invited Stanley Zuckerman and Mark Zeitz, as well as several popular girls from school for a little get-together in Marvin’s treehouse.

Audrey Rosen knew that her next-door neighbor Boychick would protect her from any trouble so she accepted immediately. She volunteered to bring her pretty friend, a very reluctant Debbie Katz.

“I'll break a nail climbing up there” Debbie whined. “And it looks so dirty!”

Audrey pretended to convince Debbie, even though she knew if she was going, her friend would follow. “Come on Debbie. It'll be fun. The boys are up there.”

Once they were all together, small talk about school and fat Mrs. Waller soon got boring. The girls were here… in Marvin’s treehouse. What game could they play to involve everyone?

Boychick couldn't help noticing how cute Audrey looked with her hair tied in pigtails.

“She is so likeable”, he thought to himself, “kneeling on the tree house floor, able to fit right in with the group".

Boychick focused first on Audrey's pink flip-flop sandals, then on the small dirt stains on her knees, memorizing and filing the pictures in his brain for later.

Audrey's adorable Jappy friend Debbie was not going to dirty her knees on that rough plank treehouse floor. She preferred the outside landing, acting uninterested in these teenage boys, calmly filing her nails.

"How about some cards?" Marvin suggested.

Marvin was obviously up to something. His mind was well suited for Chess - always thinking three steps ahead. Any suggestion from Marvin would be good-natured and always fun. Marvin was a great best friend.

"We could play strip poker."

The girls were not quite ready for that game and said so.

"Forget cards, Stanley slobbered", finishing his CocaCola, "Let's play spin the bottle!"

He wiped the Coke off his chin and mouth to get himself ready for the game. The girls looked curiously interested in that idea. Both turned to Stanley to start the game.

Stanley Zuckerman was popular, athletic and very manly for the 7th grade. None of the girls in his class minded kissing Stanley. Early in September he had set a goal of kissing them all, even the fat ones, by the end of June.

Before anyone could protest, (who wanted to?) Stanley Zuckerman placed his empty bottle in the middle of the Treehouse floor and spun it. It pointed to Debbie.

She giggled a little and pretended to be shy, but she did kiss Stanley briefly on the lips.

Mark Zeitz spun next. He was also popular in the class but had a sneering facial expression due to his surgically repaired harelip, an unfortunate family trait.

The bottle slowed, then stopped, pointing to Marvin. The girls giggled, but weren't exactly sure why.

"No chance homo. Okay best buddy, your turn next."

Boychick closed his eyes for a second to summon the spirit of his great-grandfather Rabbi Mordecai Silverman. He knew that venerable holy man was also a great success with women. As the bottle spun, Boychick's mind replayed fantasies about perfect pink lips touching his.

When the spinning bottle finally stopped, it pointed to Audrey. The other boys teased Boychick, laughed loudly and pushed him to go and get his kiss. Audrey silently watched their display of immaturity. She wasn't sure if she was ready for her first real kiss, but the bottle did point to her.

"Go Harold… make her beg for more!" Mark Zeitz was teasing out of jealousy.

"Come with me, Boychick." Audrey's slim dainty fingers with long mauve nails wrapped around his own trembling fingers. She gently led him out of the group's view… beyond the Treehouse entrance to the outside platform.

Audrey looked adorable in her simple top, jean shorts and pink flip-flops. There was something alluring about the dirt stains on her knees from kneeling on the wood floor.

There was a trusting air of confidence and calmness about Audrey. Her initial nervousness was gone. She and her next-door neighbor Boychick had been friends since they were seven. Now she knew exactly what she wanted to do.

In her softest breathy voice Audrey whispered "s h h h," noticing for the first time how sensitive and beautiful Boychick's hazel eyes were. She stared into those eyes as if for the first time and drew his shivering body closer. Audrey was still a bit scared of the unknown, but convinced herself that she was ready.

His every nerve was on fire. Audrey not only kissed him on the lips, but sucked on his bottom lip and slipped her tongue in his mouth. The kiss only lasted 10 seconds or so, but it felt better to Boychick than the day his baseball team won the league championship.

The after-effects of kissing Audrey were certainly better than receiving that little wooden trophy with the gold batter on top.

Audrey made eye contact, then gave him a short follow-up kiss on the lips. They could hear the immature boys inside laughing, predicting that Boychick was afraid to kiss a pretty girl. If the boys only knew….

Audrey took control of the situation with a serious look. Her reputation was important to her. "Handle this right, Boychick."

Audrey moved inside the treehouse with Boychick close behind.

"My friends, she chickened out just like I knew she would. The girl's just too young to know what to do. I was ready to kiss her, but she wouldn't give. Forget this stupid game. Let's go get ice cream."

Boychick and Audrey now shared two secrets that only they would ever know - this Treehouse kiss and The Secret Flight when they were much younger. She protected him then and never told anyone about it.

Instinct and example told Boychick that Audrey Rosen could absolutely be trusted to keep a secret. As often happened his mind unclutched, creating a clever daydream.

He thought to himself "You could tie her up with jungle vines and torture her mauve fingernails, like in those Sunday afternoon World War II movies. Audrey would never reveal where the allied troops and local partisans were hiding."

He could trust Audrey with the most personal secrets of his life.... Audrey would never tell a soul.

ANTS

Harold "Boychick" Silverman liked to study ants before he killed them. Killing ants wasn't about being cruel or uncaring. Boychick had respect for all living creatures, but ants in his family's clean kitchen were invaders. If they detected any human weakness they would surely bring their entire invasion force.

He would watch the “Scout” ant as it checked out the kitchen counter near the toaster... looking for today's food rations.

When the slightest crumb of food was located, the Scout ant signaled for the rest of the army to advance. Responding eagerly, the hungry ant army would dutifully march forward in unison.

Boychick was curious about these tiny live moving spots, bumping into each other, one after one, spinning the latest food report on their antennae.

He wondered to himself, “How do they know what to do? In what language do they communicate? How does one say ‘little piece of Boychick’s sandwich" in Ant?

Sometimes he’d leave them alone, watching them carry tiny pieces of seeded corn rye back through the missing grout between the wall tiles.

As a member of the Cousteau Society, Boychick felt a degree of pity for these insects. The Society's guidebook said members must protect and defend America's natural wildlife... even ants.

"What a bag of fertilizer!" Boythick thought to himself.

Most of the time, like many people, Harold Silverman was an ANT MURDERER.

It was by now just a reflex. A spot moves on the counter so you push your finger into it. A lot of spots move, you reach for THE CAN.

Boychick's mother Lynn Silverman insisted on a very clean kitchen. Her entire family respected that wish. It was predictable that even in the cleanest kitchen a hungry ant army would someday attempt an invasion. THE CAN was always within easy reach.

His mind began to consider military tactics. When defending against an invading ant army, Boychick preferred the extensive use of air power.

The situation was developing rapidly. There were now many more soldier ants moving on the counter. Those lucky enough to find crumbs and debris carried their prize back toward the small crack in the tiles.

Boychick reached slowly and deliberately for THE CAN, always eyeing his prey. He imagined the ant army to be a battalion of uniformed Nazi troops, marching through the Rhine Valley toward France. The soldiers aligned themselves in close formation with no artillery or tanks to assist their attack.

Deploying an overwhelming missile and chemical defense from his Hueys, Boychick aimed THE CAN toward the ant army in a repel mode. He somehow fused military history, attacking the World War II Nazis with missile-equipped helicopter gunships.

The full brunt of Boychick's modern weaponry was brought to bear on the evil invaders. Aryan ants stood helpless in the face of military hardware from their future.

"Die you Nazi bastards!!"

Boychick sprayed a neat steady line of insecticide across the length of the marching ant soldiers as his attack helicopters blared out "Ride of the Valkyrie".

Ant soldiers cowered in fear, choking from the gas. They were not equipped for a chemical battlefield. The skirmish was over. Boychick's helicopters had won.

The fight had been glorious. He would be a hero for defending the family kitchen, but punished if his parents saw the mess.

Boychick felt the pride of victory as he wiped dripping battle refuse off the counter with the closest tool available, one of his father's cloth napkins. His mother would never know the carnage that took place in her kitchen this night.

It was a foolish mistake to assume total victory. From the corner of his eye, Boychick saw a tiny spot move… and then another.

"Escape attempt!!! Man the can!!!"

But it was too late. Boychick had forgotten to cover their alternate exit behind the toaster. The last soldier ant turned back for an instant, no doubt swearing an oath of revenge.

Boychick sneered at the escapee.

"Screw you ant, I got your momma."

He yawned… tired and battle-weary. It was time for bed.

CLOTH NAPKINS

Dave Silverman, the father of the house, the bread-winner, woke up early as usual, ready for a full day at The Pants Store. He entered the normally spotless kitchen with pleasant thoughts of fresh coffee and a toasted bagel.

Instead of a clean kitchen, Dave saw a counter littered with refuse from the previous night's battle between Boychick and an invading army of hungry ants. Worse than the mess and the smell of insecticide, one of his cloth napkins had been used as a rag.

Boychick's father Dave was in most senses a normal middle-class head of his household. He had only a few peculiarities which made his life more comfortable. His wife Lynn generally accommodated these requests whenever possible.

Dave Silverman did not like paper napkins. At each meal he preferred a freshly laundered, ironed cloth napkin. Other family members were welcome to use them, with proper respect, as long as one clean cloth napkin was always available for him.

After many years of marriage Lynn realized it actually made her happy to clean and even iron the cloth napkins. She knew it made her husband happy. Now one of his pristine cloth napkins had been needlessly soiled, disrespected and possibly ruined permanently.

"LYNN. Come see this! Dammit Lynn, who could have been so thoughtless? One of my good cloth napkins! It's soaked with insecticide! I should have listened to my friend Max after Boychick destroyed the dining room table and caught our Family Room on fire. Max always said our boy Harold was trouble… I should have gotten rid of him when he was small."

"Calm down Dave. I'll call Harold. There must be an explanation. BOYCHICK! Wake up. Come down here now."

Boychick was almost awake, but not quite. He was in that half awake, half dreaming state where all things are possible. The commotion and yelling from downstairs didn't exist here.

Last night his helicopter air power had defended the kitchen against an invading army of ants and he had defeated them. Now his mind was far away.... far from parents, and invading ants, and cloth napkins. He was in the treehouse with HER and she was gladly, willingly, with him.

Marvin's Treehouse was the perfect getaway even in a dream. The Treehouse was where Audrey and Boychick had played spin-the-bottle. It was where they secretly first kissed.

Now he dreamed it was a lazy Saturday afternoon. He and Audrey lay stretched out on the treehouse landing, eating plump red grapes and French-kissing.

Audrey was a wonderful kisser. She wouldn't let him do anything else, but who cared? Beautiful, shapely, sensuous young Audrey.... pouting devilishly, sucking on Boychick's lower lip, blowing sweetly in his ear. This was his favorite erotic dream.

"Oh Boychick, we're in Paradise! Can you feel this? (Audrey purred softly in his ear, then kissed Boychick lightly down his neck.)

Could he feel that? Oh my God could he ever!!! Boychick's whole body was electrically charged… totally on fire! The ecstasy of Audrey's neck kisses nearly rolled him off the treehouse porch! Boychick held on tightly to a small firm tree branch to steady himself.

"**Boychick wake up and get down here right now!"**

“What the hell was Dad yelling about?” he wondered. Boychick was groggy but he knew he wasn't in the treehouse. He was still gripping the firm little tree branch.

“Where is Audrey? What day is this?”

Dave the Pants Man normally kept his temper under control. Right now he was seething. A red hot Screaming Dave was so rare as to be almost extinct, but today the species was thriving.

“My good cloth napkin, my only link to civilization. That rotten kid wiped up insecticide with my good cloth napkin.”

“Calm down, dear. I'm sure it'll wash out in the laundry.”

“You're not going to put my good cloth napkin in a washing machine. This is going to the dry cleaner. When that boy wakes up you tell him he's punished. I have to go to work."

"Yes dear."

PLAYBOY MAGAZINES

Clean ironed cloth napkins were certainly a curious eccentricity. An even more curious and stimulating eccentricity was Dave's Playboy magazine collection. Every month that wonderful secret volume of stories, interviews, ads, jokes and photos would arrive in the mail, temporarily concealed in its brown paper wrapper.

Dave never discussed his subscription. He never hid it either. In truth his attitude about Playboy was quite modern and nonchalant. Boychick's father possessed a certain degree of sophistication. To a middle-aged married man Playboy wasn't that sexy and Dave did actually read most of the articles.

Lynn was never comfortable with the Playboys in her house. She was resigned to it, but the obvious sexuality of it was unnerving. In most of her friend's houses, Playboy magazine was read in the bathroom. Her husband always stored his copies in his nightstand, right next to their bed.

When Dave and Lynn weren't home, Boychick would walk brazenly into his parents' bedroom, straight to the top drawer of Dad's nightstand and retrieve a Playboy.

Something about it called to him, begging him to look at it.

Pictures of naked girls! Boychick loved pictures of naked girls. He would sit at the end of his parents' bed staring at the pictures … memorizing them. Girls in the shower… girls at the beach with no top on… tipsy girls at discos losing their inhibitions.

Not once did he ever think of Audrey or Debbie while he looked at Playboy. Those two were lovely teens. Playboy Playmates were women!!!

Why was Dave so brazen about this? Why were the Playboys left so unguarded? Did his father intend for his son to look at the pictures?... enhance his natural sexual urge for women? What a Dad Boychick had!!!

THE THUNDERSTORM

Of course I, Langameintza, heard the storm approaching. My windows were open. Change was in the air. A gentle warm breeze became wind, then turned cooler. Sounds of distant thunder grew louder.

An old shpeiler like myself has seen the seasons come and go. When I see the lightning, I just close the blinds. When I hear thunder, big deal, I turn the TV louder. If it rains, so what? Who cares? I close the windows and wait for morning. At 70, I'm not impressed with the weather.

Always when it rains I see that mashugana kid Boychick Silverman in the house next door with his face out the window... not that I'm spying on the boy.

"Get inside, you putz," I yell at him. "You'll catch pneumonia and sneeze on your family."

Like a schmuck he waves hello with a big smile. Maybe his father's friend Uncle Max was right - maybe they should have taken this kid for professional help at an early age.

"Boychick" Silverman was nearly asleep when he heard thunder in the distance. What a lovely sound... What a welcome sound.

The eighteen year old was battling an

onslaught of pollen - the Summer allergy season. Efforts to expand his lungs created an asthmatic raspy sound. He sat up in bed to wait for the next sound of rumbling.

"Yes. There it was", he said to himself. "Two! Even better."

Two thunderclaps close together meant a storm was approaching. The pressure would finally be relieved. It was finally going to rain. "Thank God" he thought.

During the last few days, Boychick felt the pressure build up inside him. Hot, humid summer mornings... intense, powerfully bright, beating hot summer afternoons. His allergies and asthma we're acting up again, choking off his lungs. Only short puffy breaths could get through.

One local station announced that the pollen count was high today.

"No joke." he murmured

Every allergy Boychick ever confronted was saying "Hi... remember me?"

On muggy Summer nights like this Boychick slept on his back to breathe better. Normally he slept on his stomach, covered with one blanket, the ceiling fan on low, and the usual two pillows.

When his allergies kicked up, the only way to breathe was to sleep on his back, with the fan on high.

Some nights when she heard Boychick wheezing, his mother Lynn brought in a vaporizer. The steam always helped. A dab of menthol Vick's mixed with the steam allowed Boychick to sleep in peace, though it was never the deep sleep he needed.

Summer was a difficult season for an asthmatic to get through, but he was used to it by now. Boychick had survived the worst asthma attack, a serious life-or-death crisis, 15 years ago. Now at eighteen, he was experienced enough to no doubt survive the next few days.

As a three year old toddler, an otherwise healthy little pisser of a Boychick contracted both asthma and pneumonia on top of the allergies he inherited from his father Dave.

For several days his parents, Lynn and Dave, sat next to an oxygen tent, praying to the Lord Of Hosts to spare their son, while preparing themselves for the worst.

Even the terrible wheezing was a welcome sign that the boy was still alive and breathing.

Lynn's father, Grandpa Ben, became hysterical when he heard that his little grandson Harold was in the hospital. It was inconceivable to him that God should take this child.

Ben openly wept and prayed every day. He even dusted off his tallit and yarmulke so he could attend Shabbat service in the Orthodox shul, just in case his switch to Reform Judaism might be the cause of God's anger.

"Take Me, God. I'm old. I've lived my life. Esther...Esther,...what does HE want with our little Harold?"

Ben continuously recited the Hebrew prayers he had memorized as a child.

Lynn's mother, Grandma Esther, was not as traditionally religious as Ben. Her practical nature told her that this was only a test. She and Ben were being tested, the boy's parents were being tested.

"Everyone should have faith" she told them. "Harold will be all right in a few days."

She continued to cook and clean and light candles on Friday night as she always did. After all, sickness was a part of life and a part of God's plan. Esther was the rock of the family... the Bubby.... the matriarch.

Outwardly she continued the same daily routine so the family would know that life goes on. Inwardly she prayed just as hard, and in private she cried just as loud as her husband Ben.

On the 4th day, Lynn heard what was to her a miracle.

"Fwisbee?"

The voice from the oxygen tent was soft and hoarse, barely audible, but it was unmistakably Harold's.

"Mama… fwisbee?"

"Yes Harold. Your frisbee is right here dear."

The ordeal was nearly over, the boy was going to live.

Back in 1965 laboratory tests for the cause of such a serious breathing issue were frustratingly slow. Harold was nearly four when his mother finally learned from the allergist which airborne pollen had nearly strangled her son.

"Ragweed, Mrs. Silverman…. Common field-variety ragweed. I'm sure if you look around your neighborhood, you'll find plenty of it. Ragweed is very common."

This was the first time Boychick had

seen his mother so angry. It scared him.

They marched together toward an unpainted battered ranch house just outside of their neighborhood, Beyond the old farm house was an untended field, formerly plowed and planted, now choked with ragweed.

His mother held his hand, leading him up a walkway and three rough stairs to the farmhouse porch.

"I'm Lynn Silverman, sir, and your field full of ragweed almost killed my son. I would appreciate it if you would cut it all down before I call the authorities."

The craggy old farmer had lived in that house fifteen years before Suburbia moved in next door to him. It was his family's farm for several generations.

The now-vacant field formerly grew wheat and hay. Back then the farm provided a decent life. His father used to keep a horse and lots of chickens. Now the old farmer rarely left his house, ignoring that field of wild ragweed.

A gradual slight smile began to define every wrinkle on his face. Just the thought of starting up the old tractor and once more plowing his field, made him feel useful.

"Don't bust your bra, lady I've got kids too."

The thunder rumblings were getting closer. Asthmatic, wheezing, 18 year old Boychick opened his bedroom window so he could watch and hear and smell the approaching rainstorm. Flashes of brilliant electricity shone in the distance.

Mr. Langameintza, the nice old man next door, stood at his window, probably also watching the approaching thunderstorm. Whatever he was yelling to Boychick got lost in the wind. To be polite, he waved at the old man and smiled.

Boychick wasn't afraid of lightning. Those brilliant flashes told him relief was coming closer. Soon he would be able to breathe easier.

The humidity became temporarily worse, as a storm approached. From his upstairs bedroom window, Boychick followed the frantic flight of neighborhood birds, swooping and diving among the trees. Many hid under the garage roof, which their intuition told them was a safe haven.

Finally all was prepared. Nothing moved. No sounds could be heard at all. Everything was dark, and still, except for his steady soft raspy wheezing.

Ccccccrrrrrraaaaccccckkkkk!!!

The lightning and thunder were much closer, annihilating the stillness. Boychick didn't mind. In fact he was quite enjoying the approach of this storm.

Flashes of lightning exploded over the Big Field, lighting up Audrey Rosen's house. Boychick wished she was home from camp so he could share the storm with her. It always made him feel better to know Audrey was home safe.

Ever since the Rosens moved in next door, whenever this moment of true thunderstorm arrived, Audrey would be right over there, standing in her bedroom window, her auburn hair waving in the first breezes.

The first breezes were here! Boychick stuck his head far out of the window and inhaled deeply. Tree branches wavered, unsteadily trying to fight the unknown.

"Coolness," he thought. "How wonderful."

The temperature had suddenly dropped about ten degrees. Boychick was able to take several deeper breaths, the last one without wheezing.

The rain began slowly at first. A few drops

splashed on Lynn's station wagon making a metallic pinging noise. Boychick was about to warn his dad that one of the wagon's windows was open, when he saw Dave running to the car, a newspaper covering his head from the increasing raindrops.

Harder and harder the rain fell, until the drops looked like sparkling sheets of water dumped from dark rain clouds. High winds blew every piece of paper off Boychick's student desk, but he hardly noticed. He was breathing! Over and over Boychick sucked in the cool fresh air. Breathing deeply was such a rare treat in the Summer.

Ccccccrrrrrraaaaccccckkkkk!!!

That was the closest thunderclap yet. Boychick's baseball trophy fell off the dresser with a crash, breaking the little gold bat off the player. The storm was in full-swing now. Tree branches battled for their lives against the strong wind.

Boychick stretched his neck out as far into the violent weather as possible to breathe in one last gigantic breath of fresh summer storm air, then reluctantly closed the window. His hair was soaked, but so what?

DEBBIE KATZ

In many ways Debbie Katz was perfect. It was almost dangerous to think of her without having a fresh change of clothes. And when she painted her toenails pink....

Debbie was the prettiest Pom Pom girl in school. She beat out seven other competitors by wearing her mother's bra stuffed with Kleenex tissues, and by pulling her "Friday" undies slightly up her lovely teenage tushy.

Mr. Gleason, the Gym teacher and head football coach, insisted that the selection committee pick Debbie to inspire his team to greatness. That evening after supper, Mr. Gleason was himself inspired to greatness.

The next day, a very pleased Mrs. Gleason anonymously sent a large basket of congratulatory pink and white roses to the new Pom Pom squad.

Debbie Katz was blessed with the finest attributes of teenage beauty. She had perfectly smooth alabaster skin, acne-free, which she lightly enhanced with natural tones. Her feathered auburn hair formed a series of perfectly coiffed waves. She had perfectly positioned highly polished teeth with hardly a mark from two years of braces.

The beauty feature she was most proud of was her “Doctor Diamond” nose. The well-known plastic surgeon was paid handsomely to shave and reshape Debbie's original obviously-Jewish nose in his unique patented manner.

In his own logo'd Surgical Suite, Doctor Diamond filed the sides of Debbie's nose thinner, removing all bumps and ridges. Next he carved the entire top contour of her nose concave so that it gently curved inward beginning at her eyebrows, then gradually upward to the tip of her nose, in the fashion of an Irish pixie. Her semetic flared nostrils were greatly reduced and paired properly.

At her insistence, Debbie's father, Sam Katz, paid extra for the signature tiny diamond-shaped dimple impressed into her upper lip. The result - breathtakingly perfect, beautiful and totally unnatural. Every envious girl on the Pom Pom Squad begged their parents for a Doctor Diamond nose like Debbie's.

Plastic surgery can unfortunately create unforeseen problems. One Saturday afternoon in the Cherry Hill Mall, Debbie was physically stopped by two jealous sixteen-year-old princesses. The girls demanded her newly purchased outfits or they would break her perfect nose so it couldn't be fixed. Debbie reluctantly handed over the ransom - three Bamberger shopping bags - six full hours work..

"Bitch", they said, "Your nose may be perfect, but you're getting a little chubby!" The cute princesses walked away howling with laughter knowing Debbie would now diet for a month.

Teenage Debbie Katz was a mirror image of the girl her mother Leah used to be sixteen years earlier. Same eyes, same nose (originally), same hair, same height. The attitude was still in development.

In her teens, Debbie's mother Leah was a fashion-conscious, high strung debutante. The "delicate woman" her Hebrew name denotes, was an adorable only child, spoiled to the teeth by overindulgent nouveau-riche parents.

Despite her parents' wishes, at eighteen Leah married Sam Katz. Once again adored and spoiled, she quickly degenerated into an uncontrollable, unpredictable, mouthy bitch, with very few friends, including her husband. Everyone was afraid to confront this woman, which gave her ultimate control.

Due largely to her mother's influence, Debbie Katz was equally unpredictable and equally impractical. On her 16th birthday for example, she wanted to go to Ocean City. Never mind that it was 38 degrees outside, Debbie wanted to see the ocean. Her father, Sam, was absolutely adamant that they were not going.

"Now young lady, you know Daddy tries to do just what you want, especially on your birthday, but pick something reasonable! The beach in the winter makes no sense."

Leah Katz was equally adamant in all her opinions, especially regarding her daughter. She fondly remembered being an alluring sixteen-year-old nymph. After twenty years married to Sam Katz she was now a screaming nightmare shrew who could teach "Bitch" on a college level.

"You take your daughter, you lazy bastard you. You son of a bitch - the kid wants some salt air and a piece of fish you rotten bastard. My mother told me once, she told me a thousand times, Sam's a rotten no-good bastard and he'll never..."

"Let's go princess. We'll take the Mercedes."

UP FOR HIGH SCHOOL

Every weekday morning Lynn struggled to wake Harold and send him to school. Half the neighborhood could hear,

"Let's go Boychick. It's time to wake up."

"Five more minutes Mom."

Boychick was still sleepy, warm and comfortable in his bed with wonderful teenage-boy thoughts.

Lynn knew her son would try her patience, staying in his bed until the last possible minute. No teenage boy wants to jump up in the morning. As usual he rolled over, ducking beneath the blanket for one last dream.

"Where was I?" Boychick desperately tried to remember his wonderful fantasy dream as he drifted back to sleep. "Oh yes,,, I remember...."

Boychick could feel Debbie Katz gently and lovingly lapping at his right ankle, circling back around the ticklish bottom of his foot, then sucking on each toe one by one. From the edge of the bed, the soft breathy voice of Audrey Rosen urged Debbie higher.

Slowly, rhythmically, Audrey loosened the ties on her white halter-top and raised her little jean skirt up just a bit. The teasing was obviously driving Boychick crazy which totally delighted both girls.

They were slim, auburn-haired Jewish teens with bright hazel eyes, small pert breasts and full behinds. Debbie had now licked her way to his knee. She giggled at the look on Boychick's face as she began licking up his thigh.

"Can I play too?" Audrey whispered naughtily. Her full lips and large tongue moistened each toe on Boychick's left foot, then sucked contentedly. The slight musky odors of their three perspiring bodies and the hint in the air of aroused maidenhoods was intoxicating. This was Boychick Heaven.

Something ancient stirred deep within him. Boychick imagined himself to be the Volcano God in a long cloak of red feathers with these two adoring maidens praying to him, gladly satisfying his earthly needs.

"Hot lava, Debbie," he moaned. "Hot lava, Audrey."

"BOYCHICK!!!"

"Oh my God, mother...not now" he thought to himself.

The Volcano God was angry! He was not yet appeased.

"Boychick get out of that bed right now.

You'll miss the bus again."

The Volcano God's mother would have to be sacrificed. His erotic visions of Debbie and Audrey giggled, then vanished.

Boychick's ten steps to the shower were awkward and somewhat painful. These morning fantasies were taking a real toll on him.

HOMEROOM

Harold "Boychick" Silverman always thought that Homeroom was a stupid way to start the day. He was eighteen years old, finishing his Senior year of High School, but every morning, 8am sharp, had to begin with hefty Mrs. Waller and her annoying sunny bubbly personality, making sure each body was in his or her assigned seat. He hoped this morning he could stay awake.

Boychick had grown to despise the cheery way Mrs. Waller chirped, “Good morning everyone”, followed by her switch to patriotic seriousness as she faced the flag to lead “The Pledge Of Allegiance”. More than anything Boychick despised her thick dark full mustache, while his was light and sparse.

“Lucky bitch,” he mumbled to himself.

Boychick was a dreamer - anytime, any place. Sometimes he dreamed fantastic inspirational ideas that could potentially change the world. Other times he dreamed grand schemes of international espionage. He had several dreams of heroic larger-than-life tropical adventures with himself as the sun-tanned hero.

Mostly he dreamed vivid erotic teenage fantasies involving Debbie Katz and Audrey Rosen, the prettiest sexiest shayna maidels in his school.

Homeroom did have its bright side - it was his first look at Debbie.

Each morning Boychick closely examined Debbie's outfit, mentally noting the potential challenge of each button and zipper. Once he had committed her outfit to memory, he would admire each soft curl in her "Farrah Fawcett" hairdo, the mascara highlighting her long lashes, the subtle hint of applied pastel eye-shadow and lipstick, and her manicured fingernails and toenails.

On warm days the schoolroom air conditioner would raise tiny pinkish nipples through her blouse. On days when Debbie wore a skirt, Boychick would lose himself gazing at her smoothly shaved legs.

Eventually Debbie would catch him staring - his mind off in a fantasy dreamland. Boychick's only defense was to smile sheepishly, hoping she would appreciate the attention and smile back at him.

Silently Debbie's pouting lips would form the word "pervert" or "ass-hole" causing sensitive, rejected Boychick to sink lower and lower into his chair.

Debbie Katz and Audrey Rosen were the most popular “JAPs” in the Senior class. Debbie drove a white TransAm turbo, complete with white houndstooth interior, T-tops and red Firebird hood design. Audrey drove a 5-speed manual, custom-pinstriped gold 280ZX coupe.

Debbie's fingernails were usually pink, while Audrey preferred mauve. Their suburban world revolved around high school, Jewish boys, Temple and shopping malls. Except for shades of pastel, the two were inseparable twins.

They both could have easily made the school's Cheerleading squad, but those girls were goyim and dated sweaty football players. Debbie and Audrey preferred to cheer their high school team from the stands as Pom Pom Girls.

Neither girl could understand a joke the first time it was told. Their eyes would squint, forming tiny “crow's-feet” lines in their base make-up as if searching somewhere in the back of their minds for a hidden meaning.

“What??? The farmer made the guy do WHAT with the pumpkin?”

While the boys were doubled over

laughing and slapping five, the girls could only stare blankly at each other. Debbie and Audrey would always insist that the joke be told again.

"Oh... I get it now." they'd say in unison, both still totally confused.

Today would be a tough one for Boychick. He hadn't studied for the big Science test, his History report was due next week, and Debbie Katz was wearing Shalimar perfume.

Before she ever entered the classroom Boychick knew.... he knew it was Debbie. His senses first detected that not-too-subtle oriental aroma - sandalwood, musk, patchouli and fresh flowers, with a welcome hint of lemon, vanilla and leather.

Debbie Katz hadn't entered the classroom yet, but already Boychick was floating seven feet above the scratched unwaxed resilient tile floor, nearly touching the off-white sound-muffling ceiling tiles. Shalimar definitely does make an impression.

Without turning around, Boychick confirmed her identity by the cadence of her walk. Debbie strolled more than walked. Her wonderful natural hip sway caused her new Candy high heels to sound out "tap slide tap slide", just like in the movie "Grease". No question in his mind... Definitely Debbie.

Next Boychick turned to make a mental photo of today's outfit - white peasant blouse, short skirt, smoothly shaved legs and, yes, the new Candie high heels. Well worth several mental exposures to achieve high clarity for long-term memory storage.

Debbie's delicate exquisitely-shaped pale feet drew his focused attention, arousing him immensely. Boychick stared lovingly at her shapely ankles and each pink pedicured toe.

No. Not today. He must not allow thoughts of Debbie Katz to distract him from important schoolwork. Boychick desperately tried to concentrate on schoolwork and stay alert, but his mind refused to cooperate, endlessly replaying a fantasy version of last evening's events.

Grandma Esther cooked a marvelous dinner. The enticing smells and delicious tastes of matzo-ball soup, chicken fricassee and brisket with kashi remained fresh in his memory.

He was so proud to introduce his new

girlfriend to Grandpa Ben. The old man dropped his New York Times and pulled himself out of his chair to shake her hand.

"Debbie... right? Nice girl. Nice girl." Grandpa Ben nodded with approval. "You take care of my favorite grandson." As usual Grandpa pinched the young man's cheek and gave a wink they both understood. With an impish smile Ben added his usual, "I love this Boychick!"

At the dinner table Grandpa Ben sat himself across from Debbie Katz so he could clearly see her cleavage. Her firm breasts bounced slightly each time her hand raised the soup-spoon to her pink lips. Under the table beyond family view, a napkin on Boychick's lap hid Debbie's other hand.

"GOOD MORNING HAROLD! Good morning everyone."

This bubbly Homeroom heifer had to be a bad dream. He searched blindly around his desk. "Where was the soup?" he wondered to himself. "Where was Debbie?" Boychick looked up to see reality as if he was stuck in a Twilight Zone time loop. Debbie lips were trying to silently tell him something.

"Ass-hole!" Debbie mimed, flipping him

a well-manicured finger and sticking her 'Doctor Diamond" nose in the air.

The classroom atmosphere suddenly became serious as Mrs. Waller turned to face the flag. "Please stand for The Pledge Of Allegiance."

BOYCHICK BREAKS RULE #1

It was now April of his Senior Year. Everything was basically following "The Survival Plan" he developed early in his Freshman Year. Harold "Boychick" Silverman wanted to attend a good college, but first he had to successfully survive high school.

During three and a half years of high school Boychick maintained three essential rules for survival:

1. Avoid attention in class.

Other than the laughter and applause caused by his sensual daydreams of Debbie Katz and Audrey Rosen, Boychick managed to avoid being the focus of any class.

2. Make good grades.

He prided himself in studying enough to maintain good grades, which greatly pleased his parents. Studying for Boychick included his daily 4pm piano practice hour, which had become spiritual - a part of his soul.

3. Stay out of trouble.

In the world of any teenager, real trouble was always available, even tempting at times. Boychick knew the risk was too great, so he stayed close to his longtime friends, avoiding characters who might lead him in a wrong direction. Besides, he rarely cursed, did not believe in stealing and would never disappoint his family in any way.

Of the three basic survival rules, the most important of all was Rule Number 1 - Avoid attention in class. What that really meant was "Don't ever answer a question unless you are directly called on". If he was ever to participate voluntarily in class without being directly asked, the teacher would realize he was smart, then want more and more.

He reasoned it was safer to stay out of the focus. Survival depended on letting teachers believe he was an average student getting decent grades with no potential to be an outstanding contributor.

Tragically, Boychick broke School Rule Number 1 in Miss Rodriguez's Senior English class. He had been so careful for nearly four years.

Boychick wondered silently to himself,

"How could this have happened?"

Could he have been inspired by her Vassar College training?

Doubtful.

Could he have been impressed with her "Town Hall Meeting" teaching style?

Unlikely.

Could he have been taken with her very charming personality and wit?

Dubious at best.

Could he have been totally and completely hypnotized by a slim shapely twenty something womanly figure, subtle graceful movements, adorable Latina features and mysterious dark provocative eyes?

Bingo!

That particular Tuesday afternoon, Miss Rodriguez was wearing a **great** sweater. Boychick rated it eighth of The Ten Best Sweaters Of All Time.

His mind-camera noted how this great sweater hugged her upper body like a fuzzy second-skin. It's blended pastels seemed to highlight her sparkling Latina eyes.

Boychick could only imagine the wanton uninhibited beast this woman could be after a few tequilas. Funny, he had never fantasized about an "older woman" before.

As usual he was off in his personal

Fantasy Dreamland Amusement Park, imagining himself to be very cooperative for a certain Latina Dominatrix.

He wasn't paying attention... he couldn't have been. Boychick's brain at that moment was totally unclutched and out of gear. In his fantasy, he was her submissive, helpless as she stood over him in a tight black leather outfit, menacingly brandishing a whip. Miss Rodriguez wanted respect.

"Who can help me with the answer to my question?"

"I will, Rosa." Boychick blurted out loud.

Instantly the reality of a high school classroom with thirty shocked teen faces hit him.

"Oh my God," he thought to himself, "What have I done?"

"Thank you, Harold, but please refer to me as Miss Rodriguez. I'm happy to have you participate today. You're usually so quiet in class. Proceed."

Boychick was a good student. He always read assigned textbook pages, did his homework and passed his tests. Up til now that geek side of him was a closely held secret. Even his next door neighbor Audrey

Rosen had no idea.

His answer to Miss Rodriguez' question was succinct and correct... masterfully phrased with accurate references to Monday's reading assignment. It was a foolish mistake to break Rule Number 1, but he wouldn't compound the error with an embarrassing answer.

The Harold side of his personality was sophisticated, well-read, and confident - a Poindexter - while his Boychick side yearned to be a popular folk hero. It had always been a difficult balance.

"Very good, Harold. I'm impressed! I wish the rest of this class was as current with their assignments and as articulate with their answers."

"We look forward to hearing from you again soon. Class.... tomorrow's assignment is......"

"Great," he said softly to himself.

As Miss Rodriguez turned to write Wednesday's assignment on the large chalkboard, several spitballs hit Boychick sharply in the back of his head.

He swiveled his head quickly, hoping to

catch the guilty culprits. His friends Marvin Goldstein, Stanley Zuckerman, and Mark Zeitz were all blankly staring into space, shaking their heads as if to say “I didn't do it, and I don't know who did!”

THE DAYDREAM OF THE DAMNED

Another stupid school day! Would this Senior year never end? It seemed to be going on forever! Boychick couldn't keep his mind focused on Mrs. Wallers' monotone drone as she took attendance. He thought back to last night's prom dream.

Debbie was gorgeous and fabulous as his Prom date. She wore a green taffeta prom gown and matching high heels with no stockings. Her legs were extra smooth tonight. Pink glossy lips moved slowly, savoring each teasing word.

"Do you like my legs Boychick?" She purred. "Do you think I look sexy in this prom gown?"

Debbie brazenly dangled one high heel, then tossed it aside. Gently her bare foot intimately massaged Boychick, trying to unzip him with her toes.

"Oh Debbie, Debbie... That feels great!"

Mrs. Waller, the hefty homeroom teacher cast a large shadow over Boychick. She was not at all amused.

The class roared with laughter and tears at what by now was a daily Boychick "Twilight Zone" episode - The Daydream Of The Damned.

"Would you like to share your love dreams with the rest of the class, Harold?"

Boychick's first visual experience back in reality was Debbie's well-manicured middle finger pointing toward the ceiling. Her pouting pink lips mimed one of several daily choice insults.

"Pervert!"

PROM DATE

Despite all the Homeroom rejections, despite jokes that she never understood, despite her great emotional needs and shallow interests, Boychick was still attracted to Debbie Katz. Half of his brain was still considering asking her to the Prom.

The other half of Boychick's brain knew Debbie Katz was, at times, a BITCH!. It was as simple as that.

Someday she might become a wonderful mother to beautiful children. Future Debbie might help her sons with their math homework. She might teach her daughter how to softly apply pastel eye enhancement and the best method to shave shapely legs without a nick.....but for now, Senior year of high school, she was, at unpredictable times, a bitch. She might also be Boychick's choice for Prom date... maybe.

Boychick fell back on two pillows to study the problem once more. It was very late on a school night, but the question of who he would ask to the prom haunted him. This was an issue which might have a lasting effect on his entire adult future.

His Prom selection would certainly affect his social compatibility as a young adult. His Prom date might someday be his bride. Who was he kidding? He wanted to get laid on Prom Night.

Debbie or Audrey. Audrey or Debbie. What a decision! In the minutes between falling asleep and being asleep, Boychick's mind worked overtime.

Many nights he fantasized about Prom night. How handsome he would look in his tuxedo, proudly holding hands with… who?

Dad would be constantly focusing and aiming his new Kodak Ektralite camera for the perfect snapshot. Mom would alternately smile and cry, sometimes at the same time, readjusting his lapel with a tight smile holding back the next flood of joyful tears.

"Boychick, you look positively handsome." Mom would say. "Have a wonderful time."

Then Lynn turns to.….who?

"You look beautiful too sweetheart" and once again the tears would start to flow.

"I'm sorry I can't help it."

Dad would usher him and his lovely Prom date to the door.

“Go have a good time before your mother drowns you in her waterworks. Oh, and this is for later.”

In each vision, to Boychick’s total amazement, Dave parts with a new $20 bill.

“After the prom you'll go somewhere for coffee, on me.”

“Thanks Dad, thanks Mom. Let's go”......who?

Who to ask to the Senior Prom? Boychick weighed options, thought very long and hard, then started to list each girl’s special qualities. The list would decide his choice. He only hoped he could keep his big mouth shut until he could make a rational decision.

Maybe he should ask Audrey to the prom. They had been neighbors and sort-of friends since elementary school. Audrey was more fun to be with. Yeah, maybe she would be his Prom date.

He thought back to when they were seven years old, the day she beat him at spitting and burping. When he pushed her, she knocked his front teeth out with a rock. That particular memory probably shouldn't be part of this prom decision. Boychick still winced at the blood that gushed from his split lip and the pain he endured. For two years he had no front teeth.

Audrey also saved his young butt at ten years old, when he played Kamikaze Pilot on the roof. Of course to save him, she pushed him into a pricker bush. Maybe he should stick to teenage memories for this adult decision.

His favorite memory was their first amazing kiss. In seventh grade, Boychick, Marvin, Stanley and Mark Zeitz played Spin-the-bottle in Marvin's treehouse with Audrey and Debbie. Out on the treehouse landing, where no one could see, Audrey kissed him so sweetly.

Audrey could be fun. She liked to be out with lots of friends, shopping or getting ice cream or going to the movies. Audrey was a doer. Everyone liked Audrey, boys and girls. Audrey was, as we say in Jewish, "nice".

His mother Lynn always reminded Boychick that "Audrey is a lovely nice Jewish girl. I don't understand why you don't spend more time with her."

"Mothers," he thought to himself. "What do they know about teenagers?"

Mom was right about one thing, everyone did like Audrey. They liked her even though she was a JAP and drove a new gold ZX that Daddy bought her on her 16th birthday.

There was nothing phoney about Audrey Rosen. She was naturally pretty and totally comfortable with her body and her mind. Nobody was jealous or envious of Audrey.

Audrey would be fun. Yes. Maybe he would ask Audrey to the senior prom. Then Boychick thought about that lovely sexy marvelous Debbie….

REGRETS

You look at me, present-day Langameintza and see a tired old Shpeiler. I've had choices and made mistakes. Overall I've lived a good life with few regrets.

Oh, to be the brash young buck again! From my living room window I could see Boychick Silverman in the house next door, shaking his head at his own foolishness.

There are times that everyone wishes they could just stop. I know Boychick dreams of this gift. Wouldn't it be wonderful, right in the middle of saying something stupid or regrettable, to just stop… and say nothing?

I, Langameintza, have that magnificent talent. Boychick Silverman never acquired the skill or luck. To me, the right words flow naturally, or not at all..

"Excuse me. I don't know what I was thinking about." That's what you say, and you don't say any more.

"What? No, it was nothing. Never mind."

As soon as Boychick asked Debbie to be his Prom date, he wanted to take it back. He tried not to ask Debbie. He tried so hard to keep his big mouth shut, but the words came out anyway. He had no means of control.

Debbie was, after-all, an absolute fantasy - magnetism beyond teenage understanding - extremely high-maintenance. Deep inside, Boychick knew that Debbie was not his destiny. He also.knew she was a stone-cold fox, and totally irresistible.

“I'll think about it, Boychick. You know I've had other offers.”

Her next words convinced him that a Prom date with Debbie would not realize his fantasies. In fact it would be a disaster.

“Are we talking orchid corsage and limousine service? There's no way I'll go with you without a fresh pink orchid corsage and a stretch limo.”

“Dummy,” he thought to himself. “You couldn't think with the big head. You had to open your mouth…”

“What was that, Boychick?”

“Nothing Debbie ...We'll have a great time.”

Boychick could no longer handle this on his own. He called his friend Marvin to help. Marvin arrived with a football.

“Boychick my friend...It’s always better to

toss a ball when you're trying to make a decision."

"Marvin, Marvin, what am I gonna do? Debbie's a dream come true, but she also can be such an unpredictable Jappy bitch!"

Marvin had always been attracted to Debbie Katz, but never revealed that secret, not even to his best friend. As he tossed the football back and forth, Marvin's mind was tossing around a brilliant idea.

"You know you still owe me from the touch football game, and maybe even from that Spin-the-bottle game in my Treehouse… right?"

Marvin was a schemer. Boychick sensed trouble...and fun.

"So my good friend Boychick...it's payoff time."

PROM NIGHT

All the anticipation and worrying was over. This Prom Night would be extra special.. Everyone liked Marvin's idea to double-date. Harold “Boychick” Silverman accompanied his date Debbie Katz, Marvin Goldstein accompanied his date Audrey Rosen.

The girls looked stunning in their prom gowns and orchid corsages. The boys were positively handsome in tuxedos provided by Boychick's father Dave “The Pants Man”.

Everyone was excited. The girls did a last-minute check of their hair and make-up. Photos were taken. Lynn’s station wagon was proposed as their limousine.

Dave loved how handsome the boys looked in their tuxedos, but was concerned about stains.

“Don't spill anything on those tuxedos boys. I wouldn't want Mr. Shapiro to see mileage on his suits when they're supposed to be parked in his store.”

Dave pulled his son aside and whispered, “Here's a twenty Boychick. After the prom you'll stop somewhere for coffee, on me.”

Through happy tears Lynn wished them all off. “Have a wonderful time, all of you.”

Outside, Debbie carefully examined the Silverman’s station wagon. Her disapproving whine and pouty expression told them all a change was expected.

“We'll take Daddy's Mercedes.”

That night Debbie Katz wore Shalimar perfume which normally drove Boychick crazy with desire. On Prom Night the perfume enraged his allergies.

Late spring and early summer were the start of allergy season. Pollen, and now perfume were thick in the air, causing Boychick to sneeze often and breathe with a raspy noise. This infuriated Debbie.

“I am not having a good time!”

She ran to the Girls Room to pout, followed closely by Audrey Rosen.

“I'm upset Audrey. Marvin said Boychick would love my perfume. I didn't know it would make him sick”

Audrey quietly laughed to herself. Earlier in the evening Marvin had given her a small medical inhaler to help Boychick breathe. When the girls returned, Audrey explained the perfume in a subtle way so nobody could be blamed or offended.

"Marvin… would you mind terribly if we switched Prom dates? You seem to like Debbie's perfume. Boychick and I will be fine."

Audrey managed a wink to Marvin without Debbie noticing. Boychick did see the wink and grinned a huge Boychick grin from ear to ear.

RESOLVE

New Jersey, June, 1981

Harold Abraham "Boychick" Silverman and his fiancee Audrey Rosen were married in February at Temple Beth Shalom, the temple founded by his grandfather Mordecai.

Marvin Goldstein stood with Boychick as Best Man, a role he truly played in life. He was accompanied by Cousin Seymour, Stanley Zuckerman and Mark Zeitz, all finely dressed in black tuxedos with their hair slicked back and their shoes polished.

Debbie Katz led an entourage of immaculate high-heeled princesses for Audrey Rosen, all in taffeta bridesmaid dresses, with bouffant hairdos, long eyelashes, smoothly shaved legs and mauve painted fingernails and toenails.

I, Langameintza, was there at the wedding in the front row - a seat of honor next to Boychick's parents, his grandparents, Audrey's mother and father, Dave's friend the kids call Uncle Max, 15-year-old sister Ruthie and her friend Max's daughter Jennifer.

Lynn's sister Zelda sat in the second row

with (useless) Cousin Sheldon, his wife Elaine and Lynn's mishpocha. At first Zelda seemed interested in her nephew's wedding, then appeared rather bored. She read a book through the entire ceremony.

In the aisles just behind the family were Lynn's MahJong group, Debbie's parents Sam and Leah Katz, Mr. Greenberg the butcher and his wife, and Mr. Shapiro, owner of The Pants Store. Flossie Zeitz brought her ex-husband Robert.

The remaining temple sanctuary aisles were crowded with much of the High School class of 1980 including Mrs. Waller the Homeroom teacher, Mr. Gleason the Gym teacher with his wife, and lovely Miss Rodriguez the English teacher.

Rabbi Shlubowitz, who had performed Boychick's Bar Mitzvah, conducted a beautiful wedding ceremony in Hebrew and English. He concluded with a surprising "high-five" to both the bride and the groom.

"Goot chob Boychick! And you also Audrey. Mazel tov."

It's April now, a lovely spring day in this

north Jersey neighborhood on top of 1st Avenue hill. Tomorrow night is the Passover Seder.

Leaves are growing on the bare trees. The Big Field down the street, is overgrown with tall grass. I hear it's due to be cut next Saturday.

This last winter was exceptionally cold and windy, keeping children indoors. Now they have come out with their jump-ropes and their frisbees… not that I'm looking. Okay okay so I'm watching the children play… so sue me!

Lynn and Dave Silverman knocked on my door earlier. He brought grocery store Mandel bread and babka from the MacArthur Outdoor Shopping Mall. In Lynn's hand was a wonderful gift for me, a photo album of the wedding.

“This is yours, Langameintza", Lynn said, “but photos can never compare with the descriptions of a Shpieler.”

That is the finest compliment I've ever received.

THE COMPLETE CAST

Harold Abraham "Boychick" Silverman
Ruth Silverman (younger sister)
Dave "The Pants Man" Silverman (father)
Lynn Silverman (mother)
Grandpa Ben (Lynn's father)
Grandma Esther (Lynn's mother)
Lynn's sister Zelda
Cousin Seymour (Zelda's son)
Sheldon (Lynn's cousin)
Elaine (Sheldon's wife)
Grandpa Morris Silverman (Dave' father)
Grandma Raisa Silverman (Dave's mother)
Harul (Dave's grandfather, Raisa's father)
Rabbi Mordecai Silverman (Dave's paternal grandfather, Morris's father)
Mr. Langameinta (neighbor)
Rhoda Langameintza (deceased)
Rhoda's mother
Rhoda's father
Rhoda's 2 sisters
Rhoda's Aunt Ida the Mavin
Audrey Rosen (neighbor/friend/bride)
Audrey's mother (plays Maj Jong)
Uncle Max (Dave's best friend)
Jennifer (Uncle Max's daughter)
Marvin Goldstein (Boychick's best friend)

Stanley Zuckerman (close friend)
Mark Zeitz (close friend)
Bridke Miesman “Worm” Zeitz (Mark's older brother)
Eric (Worm's tag-along friend)
Flossie Zeitz (Worm and Mark's mother)
Robert Zeitz (Flossie’s ex-husband)
Debbie Katz (friend/fantasy)
Madame Chin (Owner of The Happy Canton Restaurant) and 2 Chinese waiters
Mrs. Waller (Homeroom teacher)
Mr. Gleason (football coach)
Mrs. Gleason (coach’s wife)
Rabbi Shlubowitz
Mohel Eliyahu Ben-Zion
The Curva
Benny (the undertaker)
Mr. Greenberg (the butcher)
The Sales Manager
The Furniture Promoter
The Allergist
The Farmer
Mr. Shapiro (Owner of The Pants Store)
Medical staff at Jewish Hospital
The School Counselor
A Safety Patrol (anonymous student)

YIDDISH

The name combines the German words, "Jud" (Jew) and "Deutsch" (German). It is an expressive, sentimental, sarcastic, resilient language of great charm and nuance.

As the language travelled, it became hybrid, absorbing or modifying words and phrases from local languages. It also contributed many words and phrases.

The Yiddish language was and is the common language of Ashkenazi Jews from Germany to Russia including all of Eastern Europe from the Mediterranean to the Black Sea to the Baltic.

In the 1880s and 1890s, when Eastern European and Russian Jews began migrating to western Europe and America, they added their irrepressible language to each local culture, including America.

Yiddish is in decline. It survives today in people old enough to remember. The character of Langameintza The Shpeiler was written as a voice from that past era, with hope that the Yiddish language, it's popular sayings, it's songs, it's theater, it's humor and its culture will revive.

YIDDISH AND HEBREW WORD DEFINITIONS

Alte kocker - an old inept person
Balaboosta - homemaker or a bossy woman
Bar Mitzvah - religious rite-of-passage during a male's thirteenth year
Bashert (Hebrew) - meant to be
Babka - type of pastry
Boychick - darling son, a term of affection
Bridke - loathsome, nasty
Bris (Hebrew) - ceremonial removal of foreskin, usually on the 8th day
Bubby - A very special loved one
Chazzer - pig, overeater, ungrateful, greedy
Chuch - bring up phlegm
Curva - prostitute
Doven (Hebrew) - pray
Drek - junk, garbage, excrement
Dybbuk (Hebrew) - a malicious spirit or dead soul possessing a body
Ehmes - truth
Elohim - one of the biblical names for God
Fress - eat heartily, eat to excess
Gantze - entire, complete
Gashmeer - the entirety, all of it
Gonif - thief, clever or dishonest person
Goy - gentile, not a Jew
Goyim - plural of goy

Goyisheh kop - Gentile brains (not a compliment)
Grepps - burp
Hamisha - friendly, informal, social
Hock - bring up phlegm for spitting
Kabbalah - (Hebrew) book containing mystical interpretations of the Torah
Kenahora - 3 words meaning "no evil eye"
Kinder - children, family
Kocker- literally one who poops, clumsy.
Kosher - (Hebrew) adherence to the 600+ dietary laws
Kvell - brag
Kvetch - complain
Lashon hara - (Hebrew) "evil tongue", degrading gossip
Machas - bigshots
Mandel bread - hard baked pastry
Mashugana - crazy, a crazy person
Mavin - Expert, gossip, busybody
Mazel tov - good luck
Megillah - entirety
Meintza - story
Meisman - an ugly male person
Mensch - polite man
Mieskeit - homely, plain, ugly
Mishpocha - family, entire family
Meydl beibi - baby girl
Nebbish - a weak person

Nudnik - troublemaker, annoyance
Oneg Shabbat - (Hebrew) desserts and coffee after Friday night service
Oy - n expression of pain or frustration
Payot - (Hebrew) pe'ah - "corner, side, edge" - traditional long sideburns
Pesach (Hebrew) - Passover
Platz - fall down, be infuriated
Putz - idiot, awkward person
Rachmunas - sympathy, pity
Rechilut - (Hebrew) gossiping
Rugelach - small pastry stuffed with chopped nuts and fruit or chocolate
Schlock - cheap or inferior goods
Schmear - a spread on a bagel usually cream cheese or chicken fat
Schmuck - an idiot, a fool
Shabbat - (Hebrew) "Day of rest", from sunset Friday to sunset Saturday
Shabbat Shalom - (Hebrew) friendly greeting on Friday night
Shayna maidel - pretty girl
Shayna punim - pretty face
Shlemiel - luckless fool
Shlep - carry, drag with difficulty
Shmooze - to converse, to charm
Shpiel - a story, high-flown talk, sales pitch
Shpeiler - a storyteller, a person with an extravagant line of talk, a salesman

Shpilkas - “itchy butt”, nervous
Shtetl - small Jewish town
Shul (Hebrew) - temple
Shvitzy - sweaty, very humid
Strudel (Ger) - a sweet fruit pastry
Tallit (Hebrew) - fringed and knotted ceremonial garment
Talmud - (Hebrew) revered historical interpretations of the Torah
Torah - (Hebrew) the first five books of The Bible, the hand-printed scroll
Tsimis - a mixture, confusion, a holiday dish of carrots, nuts and fruit
Tuchas - butt
Vantz - bedbug, an annoying person
Yarmulke - skullcap
Yiddish - a Jewish Eastern European common language and culture
Zaftig - heavy, fat

REFERENCES

Many thanks to these exceptional sources:

1001 Yiddish Proverbs
by Fred Kogus (1970)
#46, #68, #104, #116, #213,
#518, #544, #612, #803, #999

The Joys Of Yiddish
by Leo Rosten (1968)

Leviticus 19:16

www.earthkosher.com

https://www.houseofnames.com/Zeitz-family-crest

Www.dictionary.com

Www.thesaurus.com

Www.Urbandictionary.com

Www.yiddishdictionaryonline.com

Www.Wikipedia.org

THE AUTHOR

All of my great-grandparents were born in "The Pale Of Settlement", a vast region of western Russia and most of Eastern Europe. A large Ashkenazi Jewish population lived, worked and prayed in reasonable safety. Yiddish was their common language..

In 1881, the murder of Czar Alexander was blamed on Jews. Many Jewish families left familiar lives for a long journey and the hope of a better life in America.

My mother's grandfather Alexander Bernstein was born in Bialyshtok Poland, the largest urban Jewish population and a center for education and culture. He was named for the Czar.

In Yiddish and German "Bernstein" translates as "burnt stone". It's likely the family came to Poland from Germany and either made or sold bricks.

Alexander emigrated early in the 1890s. He met and married Fannie in England on his way to America. They had 8 children. The youngest child Martin was my grandfather.

My mother's other grandfather Samuel Schwartz was born in Grubna Moldavia. He also emigrated in the 1890s. He also had 8 children. My grandmother Ada was 7th of 8.

The family name was originally said to be Mashivitsky, but Samuel thought that would sound too Jewish in America. He changed the name to Schvartz-Bart ("black beard") then to Schwartz Samuel's first wife died in 1910. His second wife is shown with him.

There are no known photos of my father's grandfather, Rabbi Lemuel Dichowski. He led a congregation in Bialyshtok, emigrated in the 1890s and was the inspiration for the story "God Was With This Man".

Three of my grandparents were born in New York. The fourth, my father's mother Rose, was born in the Kiev area of Ukraine. She emigrated with her parents and four sisters around 1906. The Metz family mainly spoke Yiddish.

From my earliest memories of Grandma Rose (1960s) she always greeted us kids with Yiddish nicknames like mammalleh or tattalleh. I was always her "Boychick".

The first Boychick stories were written after college (1977) along with a list of ideas for more stories. Some of my favorites were written in 1990 -1991, stored on a 5" floppy disc, printed, then placed in a box.

In 2017, I found and read that box of unfinished stories and the list of ideas. Inspiration took over. After completing 38 stories I decided to stop and share. This expanded edition has added 6 more. There are several more Boychick stories that I hope to write.

The stories and characters are fiction, based on my life experience. The three stories closest to real life are The Two-Wheel Bicycle, Boychick's Bar Mitzvah, and The Red Hand Of Dave. I still recall getting spanked by those enormous hands.

One true personal fact was adapted for Boychick Silverman. My Hebrew name at birth was “Avram”, which was the Biblical prophet's original name before he saw God.

It's rare that anyone changes their Hebrew name, but it can be requested at Bar Mitzvah. With the blessing of Rabbi Emmet Allen Frank, my Hebrew name "Avram" was changed to “Avraham” on October 19, 1968.

The Boychick stories are dedicated to my entire gantze mishpocha (family) for their inspiration and support.

Richard L. Decof, is a graduate of The George Washington University (1977) with a B.A. in American Civilization (History and Literature).

The Boychick story collection completes a lifetime dream to write a "Great American Novel", or at least publish some entertaining Summer reading.

Please post a review on Amazon.com

FUTURE PROJECTS

Two new short story collections are in progress. If you write stories I invite you to participate.

For the first collection, send me an original short story you wrote about family, growing up, being clever, memories of holiday dinner with grandparents, a fun memory of childhood best friends or something emotionally moving and heart-warming.

Please... no stories about Boychick or characters in my book. I have several stories I plan to contribute. All the others will be from my readers. The goal is 40 short stories.

For the second collection, send me an original story about your vivid dream of a past life, or deja vu that came true, or a memoir of a late relative you believe contacted you in a positive way.

I'm not looking for horror stories. Again the goal for this collection is 40 stories, including my story "The Guff".

My email is boychickstories@aol.com